THE BLACKSTONE SHE-DRAGON

ALSO BY ALICIA MONTGOMERY

THE TRUE MATES SERIES

Fated Mates

Blood Moon

Romancing the Alpha

Witch's Mate

Taming the Beast

Tempted by the Wolf

THE LONE WOLF DEFENDERS SERIES

Killian's Secret

Loving Quinn

All for Connor

THE BLACKSTONE MOUNTAIN SERIES

The Blackstone Dragon Heir

The Blackstone Bad Dragon

The Blackstone Bear

The Blackstone Wolf

The Blackstone Lion

The Blackstone She-Wolf

The Blackstone She-Bear

The Blackstone She-Dragon

This is a work of fiction. Names, characters, businesses, places, events, locales, and incidents are either the products of the author's imagination or used in a fictitious manner. Any resemblance to actual persons, living or dead, or actual events is purely coincidental.

Copyright © 2018 Alicia Montgomery
Cover design by Melody Simmons
Edited by LaVerne Clark

All rights reserved.

THE BLACKSTONE SHE-DRAGON

BLACKSTONE MOUNTAIN BOOK 8

ALICIA MONTGOMERY

CHAPTER ONE

THE ALARM CLOCK CHIMED, its familiar ring-ding-ding sound pulling Sybil Lennox out of a deep sleep. Her eyes fluttered open and she reached over to her bedside table and turned it off.

"Hmmm..." She sighed audibly as she sat up and stretched her arms over her head. *What a strange dream.* Her dream was ... she shook her head. She couldn't recall all the details, but remembered feeling *really* good. Like she was floating in warm water.

Her inner dragon agreed. Whatever the dream was, it had been amazing. The creature inside her was content to just laze around in bed, but Sybil was not going to lie down and do nothing this weekend.

I'm so looking forward to today. After all, it was the last weekend of the summer and they were having the annual Lennox–Walker barbecue at Blackstone Lake.

She glanced over at her clock. It was eight o'clock on a Saturday, but she didn't mind waking up early. It would give her a chance to clean up her apartment, have a cup of coffee, and get ready for the barbecue. She was already half-packed as they would be at the lake all weekend. It was going to be so much fun, and she was looking forward to spending time with her parents, brothers, and the rest of the family.

She hummed cheerfully as she got showered, dressed in her favorite bathing suit and sundress, and finished packing. By the time she heard the knock on the door, she had just put three bottles of sunscreen into her bag and zipped it closed.

"Auntie Sybil!" Grayson Mills-Lennox greeted when she opened the door. The five-year-old boy raised his chubby arms up to her, and she obliged by picking him up.

"Hey, squirt." The scent of bear cub filled her nostrils, and her inner dragon glowed with happiness as it recognized the child. Sybil's animal was especially protective over children, and probably one of the main reasons she decided to be a child welfare advocate. "Ready for the lake?"

"Oh boy, am I ever!"

"Grayson," his mother, Georgina, warned. "You're getting too heavy to be carried like that."

"Aww, Mommy, Auntie Sybil can take me. She's strong, like Papa and Pop-pop."

Sybil laughed. True. As a dragon shifter she did have enhanced strength, even in human form, which was why she was always extra careful. "You're growing real big, Grayson." She put him down. "How much mac and cheese have you been eating?"

"Lots!" the boy said proudly.

"We should get going," Georgina said. "Luke is waiting for us outside."

"I'm all ready," Sybil proclaimed, then turned to Grayson. "Are you excited for the weekend, squirt?"

"I am! Papa said that we're going to go swimming, and then have barbecued ribs and...."

Sybil let the boy ramble on as she locked her door and then followed mother and son down to the first floor where Luke's shiny new truck was waiting in the driveway of her apartment complex. She opened the rear passenger door and helped Grayson inside before climbing in.

"Hey, Luke." She squeezed his shoulder as she moved into the back seat.

"Sybbie," he greeted back using his favorite childhood nickname. "Did you lock your door?"

She rolled her eyes as she strapped Grayson into his car seat. "Yes."

"And you have the timers on your lights?"

"Uh-huh." She patted Grayson on the head, then put her own seatbelt on.

"And you changed the batteries on your smoke detector?"

"Seriously? I'm a dragon, remember?"

Luke's tawny gold eyes stared back at her, dead serious. "Which is why I'm asking. Do you remember when you were eight and you—"

"Shush! That was years ago." She put her hand up. "Fine. Yes, *Mom*," she said in a sarcastic tone. "I changed the batteries last week."

"Good." He nodded and turned to his mate. "Ready?" Georgina nodded and Luke put the truck in gear, then drove out to the main road.

Georgina glanced back at Sybil. "You know he's like this because he cares about you, right?"

"And because you live in a dodgy neighborhood," Luke added, looking at her from the rearview mirror.

"It is not dodgy," she said defensively. "It's quaint."

"It's dodgy," he insisted.

She huffed. "It's near work, which means I save on gas, plus it's what I can afford on my salary." Her apartment complex was located in a less-affluent part of Blackstone, but it was also accessible to the highway that led to the next town. Although the Welfare Service Office was located in Blackstone, her division actually served the entire county, and most of her cases had her traveling into the surrounding towns.

"You could live at the castle," Luke pointed out.

"So could you," she shot back. Although he grunted and turned his attention back to the road, she saw the smile at the corner of his lips. Her brother had always told her how proud he was that she wanted to make her own way in life, despite all the advantages they had growing up.

"He just wants you to be happy and safe," Georgina said. "Right, Luke?"

"You need someone to take care of you," he said.

"Excuse me?" Sybil said, trying not to raise her voice.

"You know what I mean."

She sat back and crossed her arms over her chest. "You, Jason, and Matthew spent most of my teen years scaring off any boy who came near me, and *now* you're complaining that I don't have a boyfriend?"

"I don't want just *any* boyfriend for you," Luke grumbled. "You should have someone who will respect you and treat you right. Then *maybe*, I might stop worrying about you."

"Now you sound like a nosy old lady, *Grandma*." Sybil pouted.

It wasn't that she didn't like guys or wanted to be single the rest of her life. She didn't think she was bad looking. She was on the petite side, which meant every guy she met was taller than her; she'd been told she was pretty, with her heart-shaped face, dark lashes, and gray eyes; and she knew guys stared at her double-D boobs and shapely butt all the time.

No, the problem wasn't with this body; it was the *other* body. Her dragon was just too strong and powerful for most of the shifter men in town. Growing up, all the boys in her high school had been terrified of her dragon. She felt their animals cower in fear, even though she'd learned to control her dragon since she was a child. Plus, it didn't help that she was the only daughter of the richest man in town who practically owned Blackstone. While all the girls her age were experiencing their firsts—first dates, first kisses, first boyfriends, first, *ahem*, times—she had been left untouched in the corner like the veggie dish at a potluck. By the time she went off to college, she had simply lost hope and interest in boyfriends and focused instead on her career.

It didn't mean she wasn't open to the possibility. And, if she were honest with herself, she was envious of her family and friends. Everyone had already paired off, finding their mates, while she was left alone again. Even Kate—who swore off relationships—found her mate in Petros. What she wouldn't give to even have a decent date with a nice guy. Just something *normal*.

Georgina sensed the growing tension and cleared her throat. "So, it's still about an hour to the lake. Why don't we play a game? Grayson?"

"Ooh! How about *I Spy?*"

Sybil put all thoughts of boys, boyfriends, and mates aside. "Why don't I go first?" She grinned at Grayson. "I spy, with my little eye, ..."

After their huge barbecue lunch, the whole Lennox–Walker clan decided it was time for a dip in the lake. Sybil sat on the shore, content to watch everyone have fun. Jason, Christina, Petros, and Kate were all playing chicken fight, the girls on their respective mates' shoulders as they tried to push each other over. Ben and Penny were sitting on beach chairs, holding hands while they chatted softly. Matthew and Catherine were lazing on their inflatable tubes, while Luke was teaching Grayson how to swim. Meanwhile, Cassie Grimes was riding on the back of her great-uncle Tim, who was in polar bear form. Cassie's dad, Mason and his mate, Amelia Walker, were sitting on the dock that stretched out from the shore. Laura, Amelia's mom, came over and spoke with them, and when she left, the couple stood and walked toward the woods.

She was glad Amelia was back, and also back with her mate. They had broken up a couple of years ago, but when Mason moved to town, they had reunited. Sybil knew part of the story, having been there when Amelia had been inconsolable in the wake of the breakup.

Sybil was also the social worker who had checked up on Cassie when she came to Blackstone after an emergency removal from Mason's ex-wife's custody. She could have been vindictive, since Mason broke one of her best friends' heart, but she was a professional. Besides, she'd read Cassie's case file; not only had the young girl been abandoned by her mom, but Mason wasn't even her biological father. Yet he'd stepped up and taken care of her like she was his own. She had to give him props for that.

"Everything okay, princess?" Her father, Henry Lennox—Hank to his friends—plopped down on the sand next to her and put an arm around her.

"Hey, Dad." She leaned her head on his shoulder. "Yeah, I'm good. Just thinking. You?"

"Doing great, now that I'm here with all of you." He flashed her a smile, the corners of his eyes crinkling. "Are you sure you're okay?"

She laughed. "I'm fine."

"Work's good?"

"Yeah, same old, same old." Her work was never boring, that was for sure, and some days, it was heartbreaking and exhausting. But seeing the kids smile made it all worth it, especially with what they went through. "I just—Dad?"

Hank's body stiffened, and his eyes began to glow. Sybil could feel his inner dragon stand to attention, and her own animal mirrored its sire. The hairs on the back of her neck stood up, and her skin crawled. *Danger.*

Her father stood, grabbed her elbow, and pulled her up. The tension in the air was palpable. She looked around her. Matthew, Jason, and everyone else who had been swimming were walking up to the shore. When Hank's head whipped around, she saw what had sent all their senses on alert.

There were five men standing there, right in front of Uncle James' cabin. Now, Sybil was 100 percent sure they had not been there a second ago, nor had she sensed their approach. In fact, it was like they had just appeared out of thin air.

Hank's jaw set. "The kids. And the women—"

"Christina's taking them inside," Jason said as he came closer.

"Sybil, go with them," Matthew ordered.

"What?" She glanced back at the men, who had not moved an inch. "No way." She looked around her. Luke, Uncle James, Tim, Petros, Kate, and Ben were coming towards them. "I'm one of you, remember?" Her dragon uncoiled inside her, ready to protect her loved ones.

"If they need help—"

"Then I'll fly them off in a sec," Sybil said. "But I'm staying here."

"They're coming," Jason warned.

Hank turned to face the intruders, putting himself between them and his family. Matthew and Jason stood behind him, while the rest spread out behind the trio, flanking all sides.

The five men walked toward them with deliberate steps. As they came closer, Sybil's shifter instincts went into overdrive.

Dragons.

Five dragons had landed in Blackstone. *But why?* Sybil knew of the existence of other dragons in the world but like the Lennoxes, most kept a low profile. Her father and brothers never gave out interviews or allowed outsiders into their lives. As Riva had explained when they were teenagers, the Lennox Corp. Public Relations Department's main function was to keep them *out* of the public eye.

Of course, she couldn't help herself: out of curiosity, she'd done a Google search for other dragon shifters but found very little information. There was a mention of a dragon in Chicago who lived in the tallest building in the world and one that lived in England or somewhere in the U.K., but there was not much else. It was like the existence of dragons had been scrubbed from the World Wide Web and the greater world in general.

"You stop right there," Hank said. His tone was calm, but the presence of his dominant dragon was unmistakable.

The men stopped in their tracks. Sybil's eyes narrowed at

them. Each one of them wore different clothing, but they were definitely all dragons, though she sensed something was unique about each of them. *But what?*

"Greetings, Henry Lennox, Blackstone Dragon." The man in the middle, a tall, thin man wearing silver robes said. He had a pleasant voice with a slight accent Sybil couldn't place. English? Irish?

"Who are you and what do you want?" came Hank's reply.

Another man—this one short and stocky and wore an immaculate white suit—spoke next. "We are the Dragon Council."

"Dragon Council?" Hank echoed. "I've never heard of you."

"Of course not," white suit said, his aristocratic voice almost a sneer. "Your ancestor, Anastasia Lennox got your clan banished from the Dragon Alliance when she defied dragon law and *mated*"—the disdain in his voice was evident —"with a common shifter."

Sybil bit her lip to stop her gasp, but beside her, she could feel Uncle James and Ben tense. She didn't blame them, of course. He was talking about their ancestor, Silas Walker, a bear shifter who had married Anastasia Lennox.

"Caesar, please," silver robe interrupted. "That's all in the past, right? Does it matter?"

"What matters is why you're here. On my mountain," Hank said, his arms crossing over his chest. "How the hell did you sneak up on us, and what do you want?"

"We Cloaked, of course," silver robe replied matter-of-factly. "Have you never Cloaked before?"

Caesar clucked his tongue and turned to silver robe. "See, Balfour? I told you, we don't even know how they've regressed, being away from other dragons."

Balfour's eyes flashed silver. "*Please*, Caesar." He turned back to Hank. "Kindly excuse us. As Dragon Council, we put everything to a vote and unfortunately, my compatriot lost this one."

Hank looked at the men impatiently. "Will one of you just please tell me what's going on?"

"Since you are apparently unaware of the events of the past century or two, let me start from the beginning." Balfour cleared his throat. "A few thousand years ago, dragon shifters lived peacefully with humans and all other shifters; however, through the centuries, humans began to hunt us down and thus, those of us that remained formed the Dragon Alliance. Each clan sends one representative to the Dragon Council, who then creates and enforces dragon laws. These laws are meant to keep us safe and ensure the survival of our species." He paused. "When, uh, your ancestor, Anastasia Lennox broke dragon law, the Lennoxes were banished from the Dragon Alliance as punishment."

"Their lands and titles were taken, as were their treasure hoards, and they were left to fend for themselves without the protection of the Alliance," Caesar added. "That is what happens when you break dragon law."

"I think we've been doing well for ourselves," Hank said with a raised brow. "So, you kicked us out of your little club. What the hell are you doing here then?"

Balfour's face turned grave. "There are people—humans—out there who want to destroy us." He looked at the other shifters. "All of us. I know you've already encountered them and that they tried to destroy your town."

"The Organization," Jason said, his hands curling into fists into his sides. The anti-shifter group had tried to blow up the entire town of Blackstone a few months ago.

Balfour nodded. "They call themselves The Knights of

Aristaeum. Few know who they are. They were named after a wizard who sought to destroy all shifters."

"Wizards?" Matthew asked.

"Yes. Humans used to know how to wield magic, but they lost the ability over time. It's a long story, but basically, this secret society has existed for the past three centuries, and their main goal is to destroy all shifters."

"Then what do you want with us?" Hank asked.

Balfour looked around uneasily at the other men behind him. Caesar frowned, but nodded. "We seek an alliance with you. And invite you to once again join the Dragon Council."

"And why would we do that?" Matthew said.

"Because, The Knights of Aristaeum will destroy us all," Caesar stated matter-of-factly. "All shifters of all kinds. And they already have the means to do it. A magical weapon."

"What?" Hank's voice rose. "What are you talking about?"

Balfour looked around apprehensively. "Blackstone Dragon, before we go any further, we must ask that you meet with the Dragon Alphas."

"All right, I'll bite," Hank sighed. "Dragon Alphas?"

"They are the leaders of the various dragon clans around the world, and the protectors of their territory and people under them," Balfour explained. "Much like you are the protector of Blackstone. If you grant them permission to land in your territory, then we can sit down and talk about how we will stop The Knights."

"I think the idea has merit," Jason said.

"But, can we trust them?" Matthew interjected.

Hank seemed to consider his sons' words. "How do we know this isn't some trap?"

"What?" Caesar scoffed. "What would we have to gain

from trapping or betraying you? We are dragons, just like you."

"We don't exactly know you," Hank pointed out. "You show up here and then spout all this bullshit, and we're just supposed to believe you?"

Caesar looked offended, but Balfour spoke up. "We swear to you, on the grave of our ancestors, that we only speak the truth. Besides, you know how territorial dragons can be. The moment you tell us to leave, we will be compelled to do so. It is our nature."

Hank huffed. "All right. Tell them they can come. But none of this Cloaking nonsense. They wanna come here? They better show themselves to me."

"Of course." Balfour bowed. "Thank you." He looked back at the other members of the council. "Please, call your alphas."

Sybil wasn't sure what she was expecting when Balfour told the other dragons to "call" their Alphas—maybe take out their phones and text message?—but certainly, she didn't think they would all just close their eyes and go perfectly still. *What the heck—*

A strange sensation passed over her, and there was a force in the air she couldn't describe—like electricity crackling. It filled the atmosphere around them, threatening to spark and explode at any moment. Then, they all looked up.

The sounds of beating wings filled the air. The brightness of the sun prevented Sybil from getting a better look, but she could make out four large shadows overhead. Each one looked different—one of them had two legs instead of four limbs, another had scales like uneven rock—but from the way her own animal reacted, she knew they were all dragons.

One by one, they swooped down, transforming smoothly into their human forms. Sybil was taken aback when she realized that they were all wearing *clothes*. When shifters changed into their animals, their clothes didn't shift with them. She herself tended to remove her clothes and leave them somewhere safe or take them with her, clutched in her claws. But these dragons didn't need to do that. *Huh*.

All four stood behind the Dragon Council, their stances confident. It was obvious why they were the alphas. Power radiated from each of them like a beacon. And, much to her chagrin, all of their eyes zeroed in on *her*.

Sybil gulped. But she had to admit, she was curious, too. She had never met a dragon she wasn't related to. And *attractive* ones.

Like most shifters, they were all tall with muscular physiques; good-looking in their own individual ways. The one with icy blue eyes and white-blond hair stared at her with such intensity she thought his gaze would burn a hole right through her. The other three looked at her curiously, as if trying to catch her eye.

Her own inner dragon, on the other hand, scoffed and swished its tail in disdain, not caring for their attention. *Choosy much?* she huffed at the creature. But then again, her dragon had never shown interest in any male, shifter or not.

"Ahem." Caesar cleared his throat and all the alphas snapped their attention back to the council.

"What's going on? Who are those men? Where did they come from?" Amelia asked.

Sybil startled, not realizing that she and Mason had come back from their walk. "Apparently, they're the Dragon Council."

"Dragon Council? I didn't know you guys had a council."

"Neither did I."

"What do they want?"

That was the million-dollar question. "Some sort of alliance. I don't know. They—the five guys with Dad—just kind of ... appeared out of nowhere. They had some sort of cloaking tech," Sybil explained.

Amelia pointed her chin at the alphas. "And the other four?"

"The Dragon Council called them the Alphas of the different clans or something. They asked permission to enter our territory, and Dad said yes. They flew in and landed. And —get this—when they shifted back, they had their clothes on." Sybil turned her attention back to the council.

"... And so, Hank Lennox, Blackstone Dragon, we thank you for granting our five Dragon Alphas permission to land in your territory." Balfour bowed his head. "And now—"

"Four," Hank interrupted.

"Excuse me?"

"You have *four* Dragon Alphas. Not five."

Hmmm. Sybil looked around. Where was the fifth one?

Balfour did a double take. "Where is His Highness?"

The other Dragon Alphas spoke. Sybil couldn't hear them, but it looked like they didn't know or care, judging from their body language.

Balfour turned to another man from the council. "Dmitri, where is your prince?"

"I-I-I don't ... I mean ..." Dmitri wiped his balding, sweaty head with a handkerchief. "Maybe he—"

The sound of water rushing made everyone freeze. The din was almost deafening and whatever was making it sounded very big. A humongous wave cut through the lake and Sybil let out a gasp as something burst out from the water.

Oh.

Sybil's inner dragon perked up when the winged creature flew up into the air. It was large, about fifty feet long and covered in beautiful, shimmering blue-green scales. Its bat-like wings were long and delicate, but strong enough to propel it through the air. It didn't have any other limbs, but its back was spiked with dorsal fins, and its tail was shaped like the fluke of a dolphin, but matched the rest of its body and wings. As quickly as it rose up, it dove back into the water.

"What the hell is that?" Mason said. "A snake?"

"A dragon." Sybil's throat went dry.

The air felt thick, and for a moment, she couldn't breathe. A man rose from the water and as soon as her eyes landed on him, she felt the air rush back into her lungs. He was a *very* large man, even by shifter standards. He was tall, well over six feet, with broad shoulders that seemed as wide. His muscled arms were covered with tattoos that resembled scales, made obvious because he only wore leather pants and no shirt, which also showed off a sculpted chest, a set of eight-pack abs, and the deep V cut on his hips. He looked like he spent hours at the gym, but not in a gross way like those pro body-builders on TV.

As he strode out of the lake, shaking the water from his longish, light brown hair, Sybil felt the beating of wings inside her as her inner dragon flittered excitedly. *Flittered?* That was strange. It had never done that before.

"Finally," Caesar said dryly.

Dmitri took a step forward. "Ahem. May I present, His Royal Highness, Prince Aleksei of the Northern Isles, Jarl of Svalterheim, Dragon Protector of the—eek!" He nearly tumbled over when he was pushed aside.

Prince Aleksei didn't acknowledge the presence of the other alphas, the council, or even Hank Lennox. Instead, he moved forward with purpose. Sybil glanced around, wondering where he was going. And then she realized where he was headed.

Oh. Her inner dragon began to get even more excited, fluttering around inside her, its wings beating a mile a minute. Or was that her heartbeat?

He stopped in front of her, and his dark blue-green eyes shifted colors as they stared down. Sybil's inner dragon stilled.

"Hello, *mate.*"

Mine. Mate.

Sybil nearly jumped out of her skin at the volume of her dragon's voice. This was her *mate?*

CHAPTER TWO

HIS ROYAL HIGHNESS, Crown Prince Aleksei of the Northern Isles, Jarl of Svalterheim, Dragon Protector of the Eight Seas, Admiral of the Great Dragon Navy, Lord of the Barents Islands, Chieftain of the Seven Tribes, Guardian of the Moors and a bunch of other useless and forgotten titles, stared down at his gorgeous mate in disbelief. There was no other way to describe how he felt except *stunned*.

When he'd woken early this morning, he'd felt *different*. Aleksei couldn't quite describe it, except that he had awakened from an amazing dream. It felt like he was being warmed by a fire after a long, cold day. That in itself was strange to him, because Water Dragons didn't exactly feel cold, nor did they need the comfort of a roaring hearth, even after spending hours in the freezing sea.

He dismissed the silly feeling and concentrated on the task ahead. Today was the day he was making his journey to Colorado. While his wings were unable to fly him very long distances, his water dragon's body allowed him to swim for extended periods of time and breathe underwater. He swam from the Northern Sea, all the way to the Sea of Cortez, then up the Colorado River. It was supposed to be a quick flight into Blackstone town and the castle, but apparently, the Blackstone Dragons were not at home.

And then, that *idiot*, Matthias Thorne, Alpha of the Air Dragons, thought it would be funny to neglect to tell him that they were meeting elsewhere. Aleksei wanted to smash Matthias' face in until his nose bled onto his immaculate white suit. It was a good thing, though, that they were actually near a body of water, which meant he easily caught up once Dmitri had sent him the mental message about the change of venue.

He hadn't known what to expect when they arrived. There was a chance that the Blackstone Dragons would not even hear them out. Mountain Dragons were known to be stubborn, at least that's what the lore said. Since they were cast out of the Alliance, no one bothered to keep up with them; in fact, it was like their clan had simply been cut off, with no one recording their history or feats. It had been generations ago, though perhaps for the Water Dragons, it was like it was yesterday. The sting of Anastasia Lennox's broken engagement to his ancestor, Prince Haardrad, was still fresh in his family and people's minds.

The irony, of course, was not lost on him. But, perhaps fate was a jester, making Anastasia's great-great-great-great grandniece his mate. The moment he rose from the lake, everyone else faded away. She was like a beacon, shining in front of him. Calling him and his dragon.

Mine. Mate.

Of course, it didn't hurt that Sybil Lennox was exquisite. Silvery gray eyes looked at him without blinking. Her pink, rounded lips were made to be kissed. Skin as smooth as marble, but he knew would be warm to the touch. A lush body made just for him, the curves barely hidden in her short red dress.

And of course, that *dragon*. It roared back at him, full of possessive fury. He could sense its power and the fire burning deep within Sybil. His own dragon reveled in it, proudly preening at the thought that this amazing creature was *their* mate. It didn't hurt that Matthias was standing a few feet away, watching it all unfold. His dragon flicked its tail and tossed its head, reveling in the envy of the other alphas. He'd not only found his fated mate, but she was a female dragon to boot.

The silence in the air was deafening, until she spoke.

"What?" Dark lashes blinked up at him, casting shadows down her delicate cheekbones.

"You are *mine*," Aleksei said. "My *mate*. Our dragons know it."

"Mate?" The Blackstone Dragon Alpha, Henry Lennox, exclaimed. "Is this true, Sybil?"

"I—"

"Of course, it is." How could they doubt it? "Sybil Lennox is my mate." He stared down into her wide silvery eyes. "You will be my princess and will rule with me as the future Queen of the Northern Isles," Aleksei stated. "At last, you will rid your family of the shame Anastasia Lennox has brought upon you by breaking her engagement to my ancestor and mating with a common bear. You will bring yourselves the honor—"

"*Excuse me?*" Her voice rose and she seemed to be displeased.

He frowned. "What is the matter, my mate? Are you not filled with joy that—"

"How. *Dare*. You." She poked at his chest to emphasize each word. While the first touch of her skin on his made his flesh tingle, he couldn't ignore the way her eyes burned with the heat of a thousand suns. And *not* in a good way.

"What is wrong? Why are you upset?"

"*Why* am I upset?" Her voice trembled as she spoke. "You just insulted my family! My ancestors, my cousins, and everyone in between."

"Insult?" Now he was confused. He'd just offered her *the world* and she claimed he had insulted her. There were dozens of women back in the Northern Isles who would kill to be in her shoes. Maybe she was sick and delirious. "How did I insult you, mate?"

"Don't call me that," she hissed.

"You don't acknowledge him as your mate?"

All heads swung toward the source of the question. *Of course*, Aleksei fumed silently. Damn Matthias Thorne. The alpha was staring at them with those eerie light eyes, his face expressionless.

"What?" she asked, the fire in her momentarily dying down.

"*Do you* acknowledge the Water Dragon as your mate?" Matthias' voice was like a stiff breeze in the dead of winter. He was the one person who dared to not call him by his title.

"She does!" Aleksei's inner dragon roared a challenge at the other alpha. Matthias merely smiled at him.

His mate looked flustered. "What do you mean, acknowledge?" She looked around. "Are you going to force me to marry him?"

"Of course not." It was Caesar, the Air Dragon representative to the Dragon Council, who spoke up. He looked positively appalled. "My dear, what do you think we are? Savages?"

"I thought that was what you were trying to do to Anastasia Lennox?" Jason quipped. "That's the story, right? Her family was forcing her to marry some prince?"

"Perhaps that's the version you were told, but it's incorrect." Caesar scoffed. "There was an agreement between the clans. She was already betrothed to Prince Haardrad, and she broke dragon law by running away from the engagement without so much as a by-your-leave."

"But you don't forbid dragons from mating with other shifters?" Matthew asked.

"We highly *encourage* matches between dragons or powerful human allies." Caesar straightened his shoulders. "After all, we must look after the survival of our species, since, as you know well, we can only produce dragons with other dragons or human mates, if at all."

"What my esteemed colleague is trying to say," Dmitri began, "is that our kind looks at the best matches possible to strengthen alliances, mates or not. When Anastasia ran away to her bear lover, the kingdom of the Northern Isles demanded justice for the insult, and so the Dragon Council banished the Lennoxes and stripped them of their title of Mountain Dragon."

Smoke curled out of Sybil's flared nostrils and then turned to Aleksei. "So, it's *your* family's fault my family was 'dishonored' in the first place?"

There was no denying her accusation, but he couldn't control his anger either. There was more to it than just a broken engagement, of course, but obviously she was not informed of *all* the details. "Well, it was *your* ancestor's fault for falling in love with a common bear."

A deep growl came from her throat, and the fury of her

dragon was evident. "You conceited piece of—" She whipped her head around. "There's *no way* I'm going to be with you."

Rage burned inside him, and he was barely able to leash his dragon. In an instant, Matthias appeared beside Sybil, his mouth curling into a feral smile. "If she doesn't accept him, then she is fair game."

"I'm—what?" Silvery eyes grew large as boulders. "Wait a minute. No one said—"

"It is true." Caesar added. "Until the female acknowledges Prince Aleksei as her one fated mate, then she is open to entertaining other suitors."

The other Dragon Alphas looked at each other, then turned their sights on Sybil.

"What?" Sybil's tone was incredulous. "I'm not—but I didn't—" She let out a half strangled scream. "This isn't what I wanted."

"If you acknowledge me as your mate, then this will all be solved," Aleksei said. Her words had stabbed into his chest like a knife. But all wasn't lost yet, not according to dragon law. Not until she formally rejected him. She had to actually say the words. *No, this was not an outright rejection.*

But Matthias turned to him with a look that said: *not yet.* "Perhaps this is a good thing. After all, she is one of the few eligible female dragons in the world. Why should we all not have a chance?"

Damn Matthias, Aleksei cursed. Must this also be a contest between them? Why could he not be satisfied with ruling his city from his tower in the sky? Stupid Air Dragons and their quest for power and dominance.

Kal, the Alpha of the Rock Dragons, spoke up. "This is dishonorable," he stated in his low, gravelly voice. His dark brows furrowed together. "They are fated to be together, and to get in between them would be a disgrace and abomination of nature." Kal was the tallest and largest of them all, nearly seven feet tall and dressed similarly to Aleksei in leather pants, though he had leather straps that crossed around his massive chest and held a gigantic axe on his back. Tribal tattoos ran down the tanned skin of his chest and arms, and crawled up his neck and the left side of his face.

"I agree," Tarek, Alpha of the Desert Dragons, said with a nod. Lithe and slim, Tarek was the quietest and most secretive of the alphas. His eyes were the color of bright Saharan sand, a contrast to his dark tawny skin. "But, I also agree that the lady has a right of refusal, and she may choose whoever she wants, fated mate or not."

Matthias turned to the last alpha. "Your Grace?"

Ian Henry Alastair MacGregor, Duke of Rothschilde and Alpha of the Silver Dragons, chuckled. "Don't be throwing my title around like that, Matthias. They'll think me fancier than I am." His Scottish brogue wasn't as pronounced as it usually was, though he added just enough to make himself sound charming. Of course, when he wanted to assert his dominance, he used the upper-class English accent from his mother's side. "She's a fine lass. Perhaps I'll be throwing my hat into the ring."

Aleksei's dragon roared in fury at Matthias, Ian, and Tarek. "How dare you all try to lay claim to what is mine? Do I even attempt to try and take your hoards and—"

"Shut up!" Sybil held up her hands. "I'm not a prize to be won."

"I agree." So did his dragon, who nodded enthusiastically. "Because you are already mine."

"No, I am not!" Sybil stamped her foot like a petulant child. "This is insane. I don't want a mate and I don't want suitors.

I'm going to the cabin." She wagged a finger at him. "Don't even try to follow me. You—all of you—stay away from me." She stormed off, disappearing into the log cabin behind her with a loud slam of the door.

Aleksei turned to Henry Lennox. "You must talk sense into your daughter."

"Oh no." The Blackstone Dragon shook his head and held his hands up. "Do you know how many times I've tried to persuade her to do anything? Too many. When Sybil sets her mind on something, there's no stopping her."

Damn stubborn Mountain Dragon. He looked to his mate's brothers, hoping maybe that they would see reason. While the two men were identical, they gave him two different expressions. One looked at him curiously, while the other crossed his arms over his chest and scowled at him.

"Look," Henry said, wiping a hand down his face. "While my daughter's love life is a fascinating subject, I think we better get back to the real business in hand. You said that we needed to band together to stop The Knights of Ari-Ariste—"

"Aristaeum," Dmitri provided.

"Right. The Knights of Aristaeum. They want to kill all of the shifters in the world and they have some weapon that can help them, yes?"

"Yes," Caesar answered. "You have tangled with them before, so you know their ways. If we were all to fight together, we can stop them."

"What is this weapon?" Henry asked.

The Dragon Council turned to Aleksei. He clenched his teeth tight together. "They have The Wand. The Wand of Aristaeum."

"And what does this wand do?"

Aleksei's blood turned cold, and for a moment, images

flashed in his mind. A limp body on the floor. Cold, dead eyes. The wails and cries. "The wand separates a man from his animal."

Henry's eyes began to glow, signaling that his dragon was surfacing. "It turns a shifter into a human?"

Aleksei swallowed hard. "In a way."

"It makes us easy to kill." It was Matthias who spoke, and for a moment, his dragon's fury matched Aleksei's. "Once a shifter is separated from their animal, they become weak and vulnerable as a human."

Henry looked at his sons in disbelief. "This is ... a lot to think about."

"Magic, wizards, wands." One of the Blackstone Dragon's sons shook his head. "I don't know where to begin."

"So, will you join us?" Dmitri asked.

Henry paused, then took a deep breath. "I'm willing to hear you out. You will tell me everything that you know, so we can come to a decision."

"There is no time for this," Aleksei said, his hands curling into fists at his sides.

"We will need to plan," Henry said. "Once you convince me that there is a threat—"

"We have already lost a lot," Aleksei interrupted. "We must act now."

The Blackstone Dragon rose up to full height, his chest puffing out in challenge. "I nearly lost my son and my entire town to these bastards. What have you lost?"

"We have lost the Ice Dragons." Aleksei's voice was tight with barely contained fury. "An entire clan of dragons, obliterated. Not to mention the men, women, and children under their protection. Hundreds of lives lost."

Henry's face faltered. "I didn't—" He shook his head. "I will need some time to talk to my family. Let's convene in forty-eight hours."

The Dragon Council members and the alphas looked at each other, convening silently through their mind links.

Your Highness, are you all right? came Dmitri's question in his head. As dragons of the same clan and kind, they were able to communicate without words.

I am, he replied. *But my patience is wearing thin.*

As is all of ours. Dmitri looked at the other council members and alphas. *But it seems we have no choice.*

You may be right. We are stronger together than apart. Aleksei had been one of the supporters of the idea to approach the Blackstone Dragons. *What do you think the others are saying?*

I think they are coming to the same conclusion.

When Caesar and the other council members nodded, Dmitri broke off their mind link. The council members whispered amongst themselves, and then turned back to Henry Lennox.

"We accept," Dmitri said. "If you allow us to stay in your town's borders, then we will not have to travel so far."

"Fine. You may stay in Blackstone town. But," his gaze turned to Aleksei and Matthias, "if I hear of anything from anyone about you misbehaving or disrespecting *any* human or shifter in my town, I'll kick you all out."

"Of course." Dmitri bowed his head. "Thank you for generosity."

"Now, get out of my sight and out of my lake."

The command of the alpha to leave his territory was difficult to ignore. To another alpha it was an irritation; like an itch. But to other shifters, it was a compelling order. It made the Dragon Council members uncomfortable, to the point of pain. Sensing Dmitri's distress, Aleksei cloaked himself, and bid him to do the same. They both shifted into their dragon form, and Aleksei's dragon flapped its wings and lifted off the ground. While it would have been easier to leave by water, Henry Lennox's command had to be followed *literally*.

Go find us some suitable lodgings, he commanded Dmitri. *Send me the location as soon as you can.*

As you wish, Your Highness. Dmitri's dragon bowed its head. *But where are you going?*

To take care of other business. He flapped his wings and veered away from the rest of the dragons.

If Sybil Lennox thought he would be giving up easily, she was mistaken. He would find a way to convince her to see reason. His dragon nodded in agreement. There was no way any other man or dragon would lay claim to what was *his*.

CHAPTER THREE

"The nerve!" Sybil stomped into the cabin and then slammed the door behind her. "Who the hell do they think they are?"

"Sybil?" Riva, who was closest to her from where she sat on the recliner, stood up and went to her side. "What's the matter, honey?"

She let out a guttural, annoyed sound. "It's that stupid, idiotic…" Oh God, she couldn't even say his name, that's how annoyed she was.

The door flung open again, and Amelia and Kate walked in.

"Sybil, are you okay?" Amelia rushed to her side and put an arm around her.

"What happened?" Christina asked. She was sitting on the couch with Penny, Georgina, and the two kids.

"Hoooo boy!" Kate rubbed her hands together. "Where to begin?"

"Shut up, Kate!" Sybil put up her hands. "No one needs to hear it."

"Are you fu—" Georgina and Amelia gave the she-wolf

disapproving looks, "fudging kidding me?" Kate cackled. "Everyone here *has* to hear this."

"No, they don't!"

"Sybil met her mate," Kate finished with a snicker.

Riva's mouth dropped open. "You did? Oh my God, Sybil! I'm so happy for you." She hugged Sybil tight. "Honey?"

Sybil couldn't bear to look up at her mother's face. Couldn't bear to disappoint her. "It's not ... he ..." Oh God, how could she tell her mother?

Georgina cleared her throat. "Cassie, Grayson, I think I saw some board games upstairs in Pop-pop and Grams' bedroom." She stood up and took their hands. "Let's go."

When Georgina and the kids were safely out of earshot, Riva turned back to Sybil. "Why don't you start from the beginning?"

Sybil sighed, took a long breath, and then told them what had happened. "...And then that *oaf* insulted Uncle James, Ben, and Amelia, then expected me to just be his mate."

"And his *princess*," Kate said gleefully. "And soon to be queen. Oh my God, my best friend is going to be royalty!"

"No way." Sybil shook her head. "Nuh-uh. Not going to happen."

"Oh right." Kate tapped a finger on her chin. "There *are* at least two other alphas wanting to mate with you."

"What?" Riva exclaimed.

"Yeah," the she-wolf chuckled. "But seriously, princess-soon-to-be-queen is a better upgrade, I think. Hooo boy, this is going to be like *The Bachelorette* on steroids."

"No, it's not." Sybil gritted her teeth. "No one can make me do anything I don't want."

"Uh, that's true," Amelia said. "But if he's your mate, there's not much you can do."

Sybil looked around her, waiting for someone—anyone—to come to her defense. But all the women just stared at her. Of course, they were all mated to shifters themselves and knew all about the mating bond.

"Honey," Riva began, placing a hand around her shoulders. "If you don't like this Prince Aleksei, you don't have to do anything. We'll support you."

"But, you can't fight your animal," Amelia pointed out. "You'll only suffer if you do. Both of you will."

"What am I supposed to do then?" Sybil asked throwing up her hands. "I wanted someone normal. A lawyer. An accountant. Maybe even a *dentist*." *Not a freaking dragon prince, of all things.*

Before she could say anything else, the sound of the door opening made her lose her train of thought. Her father strode in, followed by the rest of their family who had stayed outside.

"Hank," Riva said, immediately reaching for her mate. The grave look on his face made her frown. "What's wrong?"

Hank shook his head. "I thought this was all behind us, but …" He explained what the Dragon Council had told him about The Wand of Aristaeum and the Ice Dragons.

"We need to stop them," Christina said in a determined voice.

"Are you really going to join them, Hank?" James asked.

"I might not have a choice," he answered. "Trouble is coming for us. They've killed other dragons, and who knows how many other shifters."

"And if they have a weapon that could kill us instantly, then we need to find a way to stop them," Luke said.

"Like I told them, I need some time to think about it."

Hank sighed. "We should head back to the castle. We'll all be safe there."

"But Dad—"

"No buts," Hank said, his voice firm. "I can't concentrate right now, knowing these dragons are nearby." He turned his gaze to Sybil meaningfully.

"It'll give us time to talk," Matthew said. "We'll all stay over, just for tonight."

Sybil bit her lip. She had to remember, this wasn't just about her. Really, if there were people out there trying to murder shifters, her problems were secondary right now. Hopefully, Prince Assface would see it that way. Maybe they could put all this talk of mates aside for now. "Fine," she said.

"You can ride with us, Sybbie," Luke said.

She shrugged. "Fine."

They organized themselves, then took care of packing up their belongings. Soon, they were on the road back to town.

"Are you okay?" Luke asked.

"Huh?" Sybil sat up and swung her head back toward him. She'd been staring outside, her mind trying to piece together what was happening, but not making any sense. Beside her, Grayson was asleep in his car seat, probably knocked out from all the excitement. "I'm fine."

"Really? You don't seem fine."

"Didn't you say you wanted someone to take care of me?" she shot back.

Luke let out a grunt but kept his eyes on the road.

Beside him, Georgina was trying to hide her grin by covering her mouth, but the mirth in her eyes was evident. "A dragon prince sounds like he'll be able to take care of Sybil."

A strangled growl seemed to come from Luke's mouth, but

he cleared his throat. "Sybbie, if you don't want this guy, then you don't have to do anything ... with him."

Sybil should be grateful Luke was standing up for her, but why did she want to rebel against him now? She felt like a toddler, wanting to do the exact opposite of what her parents told her to do.

Georgina let out a sigh. "Luke, Sybil's a big girl. An *adult*," she pointed out. "She can do *anything* she wants. With *whomever* she wants."

"That's what I'm afraid of," Luke muttered under his breath.

Sybil felt a blush creeping up her cheeks. She hadn't even thought of *that*. Sex. Despite being an arrogant bastard, she couldn't deny that Aleksei was hot and built like some kind of sea sex god. All muscles and tattoos ... not the usual type she was attracted to, but she'd have to be dead to not notice how sexy he was.

She stifled a groan. She would just have to stay away from him. And remind herself that there was so much more at stake now.

Soon they arrived at the castle, and Luke pulled up to the front door. As they got out of the car, she couldn't help but feel like someone was watching her. But not in a bad way. A thrill ran up the back of her legs, and she spun around. But there was no one there. Her dragon did that fluttering thing again and she shushed it and told it to calm down.

Get through the weekend, she told herself. Maybe she'll wake up and it'll be Monday morning and this would all have been some crazy dream.

Unfortunately for Sybil, it was *not* a dream. She woke up Sunday morning in her old bed at Blackstone Castle. Things had been tense last night, and even in the spacious old castle, it was like there wasn't enough space with everyone on edge. There was a lot of discussion on what to do about the council and the alphas, but everyone agreed that they had to do *something* to stop the threat. Sybil was just glad that it took the attention off her, though once in a while, she could feel her mother or one of the other women give her concerned looks.

Of course, her own dragon was giving her a hard time. The darned thing wouldn't stop clawing and whining at her. Worst of all, images of Aleksei rising from the lake in nothing but his leather pants kept popping into her brain. An unfamiliar tingling between her legs and tightening of her nipples unnerved her, and her dragon was relishing it all. Despite her current *virgo intacta* state, she'd apparently been harboring a horndog—er, horn-dragon?—inside her. It kept sending her images of what it would be like to be with him, his body covering hers, those lips kissing hers and making its way down—

This was not good. It wasn't like she was saving herself for marriage, but the thought of her first time with Prince Aleksei felt right, and it was a disturbing thought that she could want someone after spending two minutes with them.

Sybil had just about had enough. She wanted to go back to her mundane, normal life. She got out of bed, then got showered and dressed.

"I'm going out," she announced as she walked into the common dining room of the west wing of the castle. This section housed the private apartments of the Lennox siblings, while Mom and Dad had the entire east wing to themselves.

Matthew, Jason, her father, mother, Kate, Amelia, and Mason were sitting around the dining table.

"What do you mean, 'out'?" Hank's brows furrowed together.

"I'm getting brunch with Dutchy." *Once she says yes after I send her a text*, she added silently. They'd been trying to get together for the last couple of weeks anyway. Dutchy was, after all, the only other single shifter in their circle of friends.

"We have breakfast here." Matthew gestured to the large spread on the table, most likely prepared by their housekeeper, Meg.

"I know, but I've already made plans. We'd set it up weeks ago." She bit her cheek at the lie. Technically a half-truth.

"Sybil," Hank began, "you should really stay—"

"Hank." Riva put a gentle hand on her husband's forearm, but gave him a stern look before turning back to Sybil with a sweet smile. "Have a good time, sweetie, and say hi to Dutchy."

"I haven't seen Dutchy in ages either," Kate said. "I should come with you."

Sybil saw Kate give Amelia a gentle nudge, then what was probably a not-so-gentle kick in the shins under the table, based on the wince on her face. "Uh, yeah, me too," Amelia added, then flashed Kate a dirty look. "Why don't I join you?" She gave Mason an apologetic look.

"Great, I'll drive. I'll grab my keys and meet you downstairs, yeah?"

Sybil rolled her eyes. "All right."

Since she was already dressed to go, Sybil went downstairs to wait for her friends. She sent a quick text to Dutchy, and thankfully, she had already replied yes as Kate pulled up to the driveway.

"I know what you guys are doing," she said to Kate as the three of them drove to town.

"Oh, yeah, what?"

"You guys are being all protective," she said. "Why the heck does everyone think I'm some fragile thing that has to be taken care of all the time? I'm a dragon, for Pete's sake."

"First of all," Kate said. "If what those dragons are saying is true, we all need to stick together. What if one of those Knight guys jumps out of the bushes and zaps you with that wand?"

Sybil chewed on her lip. She hated to admit it, but Kate was right. Any one of them could be a target.

"It's best we stick together," Amelia said.

"Plus, I don't want to miss any fireworks," Kate added with a gleeful cackle.

"Fireworks?" Sybil asked, confused.

"Do you think Prince Aleksei's going to be swatted away like a fly?" Kate slowed down as they approached a curve. "He's a dragon. And a prince."

"And an alpha," Amelia added.

"Exactly," Kate finished. "He's not going to give up. I bet, the moment you step into town, he'll know it and come panting after you."

"What?" Sybil asked in an incredulous voice. "You're insane."

"He's your mate, Sybil. You may not know what that means, but you will."

Sybil crossed her arms and sank back against the seat. "You're both crazy."

"Why are you denying him?" Amelia asked. "You've met him for five minutes."

"Yeah, and in those five minutes, he insulted our family,"

Sybil said. "He's an arrogant SOB who thinks the world revolves around him and his whims."

"You don't even know him," Kate said.

"And that whole thing with Silas and Anastasia was generations ago." Amelia rolled her eyes. "This isn't the Hatfields and McCoys, you know. Besides, wouldn't it be cool if you guys did settle some kind of feud?"

"Ha ha. Very funny." But her friends' words did make her pause. What was it about Prince Aleksei that rubbed her wrong? Maybe she was being too quick to judge. "Look, we've got other things to worry about. Maybe we can put aside this whole mate thing until we've taken care of The Knights. I'm sure we can all be adults and control ourselves."

A look passed between Kate and Amelia, one that said, *yeah, right.*

"It'll all be fine," she assured them. "They'll have the meeting tomorrow, and we'll figure something out. Maybe I won't even have to see him until all of this is over."

It took about half an hour to drive from the castle all the way to Main Street in Blackstone town. Sybil and Dutchy agreed on Rosie's Bakery and Cafe. Being a Sunday morning, it was busy, which was a good thing Dutchy was already there to save them a table by the time the trio had arrived.

"Dutchy, nice to see you," Kate exclaimed, pulling the petite redhead in for a hug.

"Nice to see you girls, too," she replied. Duchess "Dutchy" Forrester was a fox shifter who was originally from New York. She had come to visit her aunts—one of whom was Rosie, the owner of the cafe—and decided afterwards to relocate to Blackstone.

Kate sat in the empty chair across from the fox shifter. "I really need to come see you at your studio so we can talk about my wedding dress." Dutchy was also a fashion designer, and she'd done almost all of their friends' wedding gowns in the last couple of months.

"Sure, whenever you're free," Dutchy said.

"And maybe one for me, too?" Amelia suddenly added.

Three pairs of eyes turned to the bear shifter.

"What?" Sybil squealed.

"Congratulations," Dutchy said.

"Maybe we can make it a double wedding," Kate laughed. "When did this happen? Why didn't you tell us?"

"Well, there was so much excitement yesterday, I didn't know when I was supposed to tell you guys," Amelia said.

"This is great," Kate said. "I'm glad. I mean, I know I was kinda hating on Mason a lot, but I know now he's a good guy."

"Thank you, Kate."

"I'm so happy for you and Mason." Sybil smiled brightly at Amelia. "At least that's one more good thing we can talk about today."

"Wait, what's going on?" Dutchy's delicate brows furrowed together. "Did I miss something?"

Sybil groaned. "It's not anything important."

Amelia laughed. "Not important? You met your mate yesterday."

Dutchy's eyes went wide. "You did? Oh, my Lord. Tell me what happened."

"There's more to it than that," Sybil sighed, then began to relay what had transpired the day before, keeping her voice low just in case. After all, though they hadn't agreed to keep it a secret, if someone overheard them and started spreading rumors, it might cause a panic through the town. "… and so, the Dragon Alphas will be meeting with everyone tomorrow to figure out what to do."

"Way to go on glossing over the most important part, Sybil." Kate turned to Dutchy. "One of those alphas is Sybil's mate."

Dutchy placed her chin in her palms. "Tell me more."

"Well, he rose up from the lake, wearing nothing but leather pants, looking like a cross between a rock star and a sex God, then walked over to Sybil and proclaimed her as his mate and future queen."

"*Kate*," Sybil groaned.

Dutchy dropped her fork onto her plate with a loud clatter. "What do you mean, *queen*?"

"Oh, did we forgot to mention that?" Kate snickered. "Sybil's mate is also a prince."

"A prince? A real prince?" Dutchy asked.

"Yeah," Kate said.

"An arrogant and conceited prince," Sybil added. "Who thought I would just fall into his arms because he said so."

"So, he's *not* your mate?" Dutchy asked, her brows drawing together.

Sybil opened her mouth, but nothing came out. Her dragon roared in protest, and seemed to take control of their body, preventing her from denying it. She shut her mouth so hard, her teeth rattled. *Stupid dragon!* The animal just flicked its tail and shook its head.

"So, you're going to be a princess?" Dutchy asked. "That's so romantic. I mean, what girl doesn't want to be a princess?"

"Not Sybil, apparently," Kate said.

"Yeah, that's not what she wrote in her essay in third grade," Amelia guffawed.

"Amelia," Sybil groaned. "Don't you dare tell that story!"

"Well, now you have to," Dutchy said.

"What story?" Kate added. "Why don't I know this?"

Amelia looked around. "Sybil made me promise not to tell anyone."

"I'm still holding you to that pinky promise."

"You have to tell it now!" Kate said. "I swear to God, I'm going to hack into your email." When neither Sybil nor Amelia said anything, she pouted. "How dare you keep secrets from me!" Tears began to form at the corner of her eyes. "I thought we were friends. I thought you guys *loved* me."

Amelia looked stricken. "Sybil..."

Sybil's gaze ping-ponged from Amelia to Kate, who was now dabbing at the corner of her eyes with a napkin. "Fine. Go ahead." She crossed her arms under her chest.

"Well," Amelia began. "When we were in Miss Wyatt's class, we were supposed to write what we wanted to be when we grew up. I put in architect, of course," she said smugly. "And Sybil put down—"

Sybil groaned and then banged her head on the table.

"Escort."

"What?" Dutchy said.

"Seriously?" Kate exclaimed, the tears of sadness disappearing from her eyes. They were soon replaced by tears of mirth. "Escort? *You*, Sybil?"

"Stop!" she said, her face turning aflame. "I thought *escort* meant you went on dates! Meg would sometimes turn on some trashy soap opera on TV while she was in the kitchen, and I would sneak in and watch it. That's where I got the idea from."

Amelia chuckled. "Needless to say, Miss Wyatt called in Aunt Riva. She was so embarrassed."

"Not as much as I am right now," Sybil muttered. "I'm glad you all are having fun at my expense."

"Aww, c'mon, Sybil." Kate nudged her affectionately. "You

have to admit, even you didn't think you'd have a prince for a mate."

"Yeah," Amelia added. "And he's hot too."

"So ... this prince," Dutchy began, her eyes narrowing, "is he super tall and good-looking?"

"Yeah," Kate said, then covered her mouth. "Don't tell Petros I said that. But really, you'd have to be some kind of monk not to notice."

"And," the fox shifter continued, "does he have broad shoulders and kind of an arrogant swagger."

"Exactly," Sybil said. "About the swagger, I mean."

"And does he have long brown hair, blue-green eyes, and tattoos down his arms like scales?"

"Wow, that's super specific, Dutchy," Kate said. "How do you know?"

"Because I think he's coming over here right now."

"What?" Sybil squeaked. *Oh no.* Slowly, she turned around, then let out a groan. It was Aleksei, and he was walking right toward them, a determined look on his face.

"At least he's wearing a top today," Amelia said under her breath.

If you could call it that, Sybil thought to herself. Aleksei was wearing a dark leather vest, which gave tantalizing views of his chest and showed off his arms. His hair was dry today and fell down to his shoulders, and Sybil couldn't help but wonder what it would feel like between her fingers. And those eyes, a mesmerizing shade of blue-green that reminded her of the sea, seemed to look straight into her. Her dragon perked up in excitement at the sight of Aleksei.

Mine. Mate.

The force of his dragon's power as it roared in reply would have knocked her over if she wasn't sitting down. Even his animal seemed haughty and demanding, as if telling her, *how dare you deny me?*

"What are you doing here?" Sybil bit out. The words sounded harsher than she wanted it to, and her dragon admonished her for using such a tone with their mate. *Pipe down, you!*

"I'm here for you," he said, his voice low and silky as his eyes traveled down from her face and over her body.

She felt the heat spike in her belly but promptly ignored it. "How did you know I was here? Wait—are you following me?"

"Of course," he said matter-of-factly. "I must protect you from all threats."

"Since when have you been following me?" She still couldn't believe it.

"Since you left last night," he stated.

"But I've been at home."

"I know."

Her jaw dropped. "So, you were creeping around the castle?" Oh my God. "How the heck did no one see you?" Luke was out patrolling around the grounds last night, and surely would have seen Aleksei.

"I was Cloaked, of course."

Oh God, this was too much. "Well, you need to stop following me around."

Aleksei clenched his teeth. "Why do you keep denying what is inevitable? I'm your mate." He ran his fingers through his hair. "This is preposterous. I should not even have to pursue you."

His words made anger rise in her. *He really was a conceited ass!* "Then stop and stay away from me."

There was a flash of outrage in his eyes. "That is out of the question."

"Maybe you should listen to her, Aleksei," a drab voice interrupted. "If she doesn't want you, she doesn't have to be with you."

Aleksei's entire body tensed and a frown spread over his face. "What are you doing here, Matthias?"

The other alpha's face remained cool and impassive. "I'm having brunch."

"We both are," said another voice. It was that other alpha, the one with the Scottish accent. "Ladies, good morning," he said, a smile spreading over his handsome face. He ran a hand through his dark hair, tousling it and giving it that "just rolled out of bed" look. "Ian MacGregor, Alpha of the Silver Dragons of Avermore."

"Good morning, ladies," Matthias began. "I'm afraid we weren't formally introduced yesterday. I'm Matthias Thorne, Alpha of the Air Dragons of Chicago. You all look lovely today, especially you, Sybil."

Aleksei's hands turned to fists at his side. "I swear to the Gods, Matthias, if you dare get in my way—"

"You'll what, Aleksei?" Matthias challenged. "We've all heard that she did not accept your mating."

"She has *yet* to," Aleksei corrected.

"*She* is sitting right here," Sybil interjected.

Someone clearing their throat made them all stop and turn their heads.

"Are you all sitting together?" Rosie asked, hands on her hips.

"No—" But it was too late. Aleksei quickly commandeered the empty seat to Sybil's right. Matthias frowned, but sat himself next to Aleksei as Sybil muttered introductions to her friends. Meanwhile, the Scottish alpha walked over to the other side and sat next to Dutchy.

"Why, hello lass. I don't think I've seen you before," he said, leaning toward her and flashing her a grin. "What's yer name?"

Dutchy raised a brow. "I'm Duchess Forrester. Dutchy for short," she said with a shrug.

"Ah, a Duchess, that's perfect isn't it," he drawled in his Scottish burr. "I'm looking for a Duchess."

"Really?" Dutchy cocked her head to the side. "And why is that?"

"I'm a Duke, don't ye know?" He wiggled his eyebrows at her and Dutchy giggled. "My, aren't ye a sight. And ye've beautiful hair. Gorgeous color." He eyed Dutchy's coppery red locks, which was styled in waves around her heart-shaped face and made her look like a '50s movie star. "Ye wouldn't happen to have a little Scottish in ye, by chance?"

"Uh, I don't think so?"

"Would ye like one, lass?" he asked in a light-hearted tone.

Dutchy burst out laughing, then covered her mouth quickly. Even Kate giggled and Amelia grinned.

Sybil rolled her eyes. These alphas sure were *something*. Speaking of which ... "Will you two quit it, please?" she muttered to Aleksei and Matthias. The two alphas were staring at each other with such intensity, she could feel their barely-leashed animals hissing at each other. In fact, everyone around them felt it, and nearly every shifter in the room was looking at them.

They broke off eye contact at the same time, then leaned back on their chairs. "Why are you here?" Aleksei asked.

"I heard this was the best place for food," Matthias drawled.

"Why did you not have breakfast in your suite?" Aleksei said. "You do have the best suite in the Blackstone Hotel."

"Are you still sore you didn't get the presidential suite?" Matthias asked. "I'm sure whatever room they put you in is better than that hovel you live in on your dinky little island," he scoffed.

"You guys are staying at the Blackstone Hotel?" Kate asked.

"Your alpha said we could stay in town," Matthias said.

"I don't see why you needed the suite and an entire floor to yourself," Aleksei grumbled. "You only did it to show off."

"Oh, is it my fault you Water Dragons can't fly fast and therefore came too late?" Matthias asked, then turned to Sybil. "You know, Air Dragons are known for their superior flying ability."

"And for being greedy and power-hungry," Aleksei added.

"We're dragons," Matthias said. "We all covet *something*."

The look he gave Sybil made her shiver. Aleksei noticed her reaction and he scowled. She cleared her throat, trying to find some way to change the subject. "So, you're an Air Dragon? And you're a Water Dragon?" she asked Aleksei.

He nodded. "Yes."

"How many other dragon types are there?" Kate asked.

"Well," Matthias began. "His Grace," he motioned to Ian, "is Alpha of the Silver Dragons. Then Kal, he was the one with that gigantic axe strapped to his back, is Alpha of the Rock Dragons, while Tarek is Alpha of the Desert Dragons."

And of course, there was—were—the Ice Dragons, but Sybil didn't ask about them. It was a somber subject after all.

"Wait, if there are different kinds of dragons, then what's Sybil?" Kate asked.

"Technically, she is a Mountain Dragon," Matthias explained.

"Technically?" Sybil was now curious.

"Yes, well, when your clan was banished, the Dragon

Council took away your titles, lands, and treasure hoards. The Lennoxes were not allowed to keep the title of Mountain Dragon. I believe your territory was composed of most of the northwest United States and Canada."

"'Tis a very big deal," Ian assured them.

"Wait, you all have treasure hoards?" Amelia asked.

"Yes," Matthias said. "We are dragons, after all, it's in our nature to want and keep things."

"Though we do treasure some things more than others," Ian said. "For example, it's quite obvious what my dragon wants—silver, though any type of currency will do."

Kate chuckled. "Oh my God, do you have like, a vault full of silver you can swim in like Scrooge McDuck?" The other women laughed, but the alphas remained silent and Ian sat back with a smug look on his face, which made Sybil think that he really did have such a treasure room.

"And what do you treasure, Matthias?" Sybil asked. She really was curious.

"Air Dragons crave only one thing," Aleksei said. "Power."

Matthias didn't seem perturbed by the disdain in Aleksei's voice. "Power is everything. You can lose your money in an instant, looks eventually fade over time, you can even lose territory and land with bad luck. But power," his eyes glowed, "*true* power is the one thing you cannot buy, trade, or steal. It must be earned."

The coldness in his voice made Sybil uncomfortable. Sure, Matthias was handsome and he could be charming, but something about him just didn't feel right to her. Even her dragon felt uneasy.

"What about the Water Dragons?" Dutchy asked.

"Probably sticks or rocks, whatever it is they have there on those God-forsaken Northern Isles," Matthias sneered.

Sybil waited for some snappy comeback from Aleksei, but he remained silent. *Huh.* If she didn't know any better, he seemed like he *wanted* to let Matthias keep thinking that.

"The beauty of the Northern Isles is in its natural resources," Aleksei stated. "Of which we have plenty."

Matthias snorted. "Why are you even here, Aleksei? You're not even Alpha. Your father, King Harald, is the Alpha of the Water Dragons."

A tick in Aleksei's jaw jumped. "And I will be Alpha one day, which is why I attend to matters outside of our territory in his place." His eyes turned stormy. "Besides, you *know* why my father cannot be here. About our *guest* at home, who needs supervision."

Matthias didn't say anything, while Ian shifted in his seat uncomfortably, and though a few seconds passed, no one elaborated on Aleksei's last statement.

"Well, I don't know about you, but I'm getting tired of this 'hoard measuring contest.'" Kate curled her fingers into air quotes with the last three words. "How about we order brunch?"

The whole thing seemed like a farce to Sybil; all of them, sitting down to brunch on a Sunday morning. She stood up. "This is insane, I'm leaving."

"Please, Sybil." Aleksei's hand on her arm made her skin tingle, but it was his plea and those blue-green eyes staring up at her that made her freeze. "Stay."

"Fine." She sat back down. "But you all better behave." She opened the menu, grateful that she was able to hide behind it as she pretended to browse the specials, despite knowing the entire thing by heart.

"This is really *quaint*." Matthias said as he glanced at the laminated pages, "You know, Sybil, there are four Michelin-starred restaurants in Chicago. I could take you to any of them for our first date if you wish."

"You will not address my mate in such a familiar manner," Aleksei snapped. "And there will be no dates. She is *mine*."

"Oh, for Christ's sake!" Sybil slammed the menu down and got up. "I'm not some *thing* to be won or owned." This really was getting ridiculous. Not even her father or brothers treated her this way, and they were so overprotective while she was growing up. She felt the fire burning up inside her and the pressure was starting to get too much.

"Sybil—"

"Please—"

And she couldn't keep her control any longer. She opened her mouth, and the fireball rose up from her throat and flew out, landing in the middle of the Formica table.

"Holy shit!" Kate exclaimed as she grabbed her menu and began to stamp out the fire. It wasn't a big fireball, but it had left a singe mark on the table.

Sybil groaned. She had just paid Rosie for breaking a chair a couple of weeks ago. *I guess I'll have to get that new lamp next month,* she thought glumly. She turned to Aleksei and Matthias, who both wore inscrutable expressions. It was *their* fault, and she had had enough. "I'll find my own way back to the castle," she said to her friends. She hated shifting in a public place, but she didn't exactly have a choice. Flying was the fastest option to get her away from this situation.

CHAPTER FOUR

ALEKSEI WANTED TO KILL MATTHIAS. Well, he wanted to kill the alpha and *then* go after his mate. However, the warning look from Sybil's friends made him stay put. Besides, this was really starting to get irritating, having to chase his mate all over the place.

That first day, after they had all left the lake, Aleksei cloaked himself and waited for Sybil to leave the cabin. He followed the car, flying high above, thankful that since his dragon's wings weren't very large, they didn't make much noise or wind. Really, water dragons were more suitable to swimming, but flying short distances was no problem.

He should have known that they would all be at the castle. He had flown over it today, and thought it was quite impressive. Nothing like his palace back in the Northern Isles, but it was clear that the Mountain Dragons had done well for themselves, despite being cast out. Of course, they would; they were dragons after all. Out of all the kinds of dragons, Mountain Dragons coveted wealth most of all, even more than the

Silver Dragons. It was no wonder that even after being banished and left penniless, they still found a way to increase their treasure hoards.

Still, it was disturbing that apparently, they had no knowledge of the basics of dragon magic. Did they also not shift with their clothes? It was a terrible thought, knowing that his mate had to disrobe each time she changed.

Aleksei had watched from above as Sybil and her family went inside the castle. He guessed they wouldn't be leaving anytime soon, so he'd sent a mental message to Dmitri, who had given him directions to The Blackstone Hotel. Apparently, the council and the other alphas had the same idea, and by the time Aleksei had arrived, Matthias had already taken the best rooms. Sure, his suite was acceptable enough, but it irked him that the Air Dragon Alpha always had to have the best. Many times, he'd wanted to put the arrogant ass down a peg or two, but his father's voice always rang in his head. *You must never reveal our secrets, son. We Water Dragons know our own true power and worth, and that is enough.*

In any case, the rooms were of no consequence. What mattered was that he had to claim his mate, and destroy The Knights before they struck again. At this moment, it seemed that the latter task would be much easier than the former.

"Well, looks like fun's over," Matthias said as he got up from his chair. "I'll see you all tomorrow. Ian?"

"I think I'll follow ye in a bit," the alpha said, a twinkle in his eyes. "I think things are about to get mighty interestin' here."

Aleksei huffed. The Silver Dragon never took things seriously, after all. Despite flirting heavily with the redheaded shifter, his eyes roamed around the room, checking out the other women in the cafe.

"Suit yourself." Matthias nodded to the women and then left without a backward glance.

"Wow, that guy is something," the woman with the dark blonde hair dyed with pink said. Sybil had introduced her as Kate and Aleksei guessed she was a wolf shifter, based on the scent of her fur.

"I don't like him," the other woman, Amelia, frowned. The woman's scent was strange. There was fur there, but there was a familiar undertone to it. "There's something not quite right about him."

Aleksei had to admit that his mate's friends were perceptive. "If you'll excuse me, ladies, I should go off and follow my mate." He stood up to leave. He didn't put it past Matthias to follow Sybil, and he had to make sure she was safe from his rival's attentions.

"Sit down, Yer Highness," Ian suggested.

"I don't have time for this," he stated. "I must go and win my mate before—"

"Aleksei, *fer feck's sake, mon,* ye have the best resource for winning your bonny mate sitting in front of ye." Ian nodded his head at the three women. "Ye lassies wouldn't mind putting my friend out of his misery by helping him out?" He flashed them a charming smile, one that Aleksei knew no female under the age of one hundred could resist. "After all, two of ye are mated and understand how it is."

Aleksei realized what Ian was trying to say and sat back down. This was difficult for him, to have to ask for help; after all, he was going to be king someday and he was supposed to project power and confidence. But then again, his father taught him the value of having trusted advisers. "Ladies," he began, using his best diplomatic tone. "I would truly appreciate any insight you would have on this matter. Why does

Sybil resist the pull of the mating call? Surely females must feel it as much as the males do?"

"Of course, we do," Kate said. "But, you can't just come breezing into town, announcing you're mates, and then expect her to fall into your arms."

"And why not?" Aleksei asked. "Isn't it more simplified, the whole thing with mates?

"Duh, where's the fun in that?" Kate chuckled. "We're all shifters, true, but we're still human."

"And we're *women*," Amelia said.

"Ah." Aleksei scratched his chin. "Sybil is looking for the thrill of the chase."

Kate chortled. "Uh, not quite."

"It's complicated," Amelia said. "Sybil is ... not just like any woman, you know? She's a romantic, but also very practical."

"She's not going to fall for the bullshit men spout to get into a woman's pants," Kate warned.

Dutchy cleared her throat. "I haven't known Sybil as long as these two, but I agree. And seriously? You're coming on too strong and creepy with all the stalking."

"I am not—"

"Ye'll have to forgive my friend," Ian said, sending him a warning look. "Things are done differently in his world."

"Do you live in some type of medieval society?" Kate asked, her eyes narrowing.

Ian shook his head. "I mean, he's *royalty*. Aleksei has never had to pursue women. They just kind of ... naturally fling themselves at him."

"I do not just fall into bed with any woman," Aleksei clarified, in case Sybil's friends thought of him as a womanizer, like Ian. "But ..." He paused and tried to gather his thoughts. "I simply don't have time for such pursuits. Too many people depend on me." His father had shifted many of his royal responsibilities on him in the last few years, since he wanted to make sure his son was ready to rule when the time came.

"Ah, so you're just inexperienced in the dating department!" Kate exclaimed with a snap of her fingers. Before Aleksei could protest at being called *inexperienced*, she shook her head. "Jeez. No way you're a virgin! But, no, I mean, I'm *glad* you're not some kind of chauvinistic manwhore who expects every woman to want to screw you because you're hot and have a fancy title."

"Sybil deserves better," Amelia said in a tone that sounded like a veiled threat.

Aleksei's dragon rankled at the thought of a common bear shifter challenging him, but he soothed the animal. *Our mate has loyal friends*, he told it. *We should be glad and allow them to help us.* "So, what must I do?"

"You need to find out what she likes and then take interest in her. Real interest," Dutchy said.

"And what would that be?"

"Ha!" Kate slapped a hand on the table. "If we told you, that would be cheating."

"Cheating?"

Kate and Amelia looked at each other. "Cheating you and her of the fun," Kate clarified. "Listen, just try to get to know her, you know? Find out what makes her tick."

"Fate or nature or God or whatever out there obviously thought you were compatible," Amelia added. "But, you'll have to find your way to being mates. Together."

"It's hard to explain," Kate said. "But you should trust us on this."

Aleksei's brows furrowed. Surely, it couldn't—shouldn't be this hard. But then again, no prize worth winning was easy to get. He was not afraid of hard work. A king, after all, worked *for* his people, not the other way around. "Thank you, ladies," he said with a bow. "I appreciate your advice."

"Oh, and one more thing," Amelia added. "I would stop with this 'commoner' BS."

"Excuse me?"

"You do know that the 'commoner bear' you keep referring to is sitting right here?" Kate jerked a thumb at Amelia. "Her *cousin*."

Aleksei furrowed his brows together. "What do you mean?"

"Oh gads, mon." Ian slapped a hand over his forehead. "Ye insulted her family the first moment ye met."

"I did?" he asked.

"Amelia is a descendant of Anastasia Lennox, too," Kate said.

Of course. That's why Amelia smelled and felt different from other bears. She was part dragon, after all.

Ian let out a loud chuckle. "This is turning into a farce." He turned to the women. "'Twas lost in translation," he assured them. "Dragons are fabled shifters, while those whose animals actually exist are called common shifters. He wasn't referring anyone as a commoner because they weren't royalty."

"Fabled shifters?" Dutchy asked.

"Shifters who turn into mythical creatures, and not real ones," Ian added.

"We are the only ones who exist of that kind," Aleksei explained. "But our history says once there were others, before they were hunted down."

"Others?" Dutchy's eyes grew wide.

"Yes, like basilisk, hydras, thunderbirds, unicorns—"

Kate's jaw dropped. "Unicorns?"

"Why yes," Ian said. "Where do ye think men got the stories from? Though from what I've read, they weren't the docile creatures men wrote them to be."

Aleksei turned to Amelia. "I apologize for inadvertently insulting you and your family. I swear, I didn't mean it."

"You seem sincere and I understand how this could be a misunderstanding, so apology accepted," Amelia said with a smile. "But I'm not the only one you should be apologizing to."

"Of course, *some* do use it as a slur," Ian added. "As ye've heard from our, er, blowhard friends."

"I will think about your words," Aleksei told them.

"One more thing," Kate said, as he turned toward the door.

"Yes?"

"You hurt her, and we'll kill you." The three women looked at him with dead serious looks on their faces.

"I have no doubt." With a final nod goodbye, he walked out of the door. He appreciated that his mate had such faithful friends and he had to trust them. Of course, according to them, he had already insulted her, but he would never intentionally hurt his mate. They were meant to be together. Deep in his heart, he knew it and so did his dragon. It roared impatiently at him.

She will be ours, he assured his inner dragon. *I swear it.*

Of course, while his dragon had already claimed her as theirs, there was one other complication.

Would his people accept Sybil as their Queen? Or would Sybil even be a good queen?

His dragon hissed at him in anger at her defense, as if telling him, "Of course she will, fool, she's *our* mate." Aleksei didn't know whether to laugh or roll his eyes. They had spent just minutes in each other's company and yet his dragon was confident in its assessment.

Of course, dragons knew nothing of history, and it did not care that the broken engagement of Anastasia Lennox and Prince Haardrad had left lasting scars on his people.

CHAPTER FIVE

"Oh good, you're all here," Sybil said as she walked up to the patio behind the castle. Her parents, Uncle James and Aunt Laura, brothers and their mates were all sitting around a table finishing up brunch. "I'm going home," she announced.

"No way," Luke protested.

"I think you should stay here for the time being," Matthew suggested. "Until we're sure you'll be safe."

"Your brothers are right," Hank said. "You can stay in your old room."

"Nuh-uh." Oh no, she was putting her foot down. It was bad enough that some alpha male wanted to take her away, but now the men in her family were pulling this protective BS. "I have a job."

Hank looked at his sons. Luke simply crossed his arms over his chest, while Matthew looked lost. "You're an adult. You can do what you want, but there's so much more at stake here. Maybe you can take a leave of absence."

"No way. There are people depending on me, Dad." Her

work ethic and sense of responsibility wouldn't let her just leave like that. Her job was too important and the kids needed her. Tomorrow she had to meet with a new client, and from what she'd read in his case files, she needed to do this home visit sooner than later.

"Fine, but I'll take you home," Luke said.

Hank seemed mollified. "I know you'll make sure she gets home safe."

Sybil breathed a sigh of relief. "Great. I'll grab my stuff."

The ride back to her place was silent. When Luke pulled up in front of her apartment complex, he turned to her. "Maybe I should stay with you."

"Are you freaking kidding me, Luke?" She had just about had enough. All this testosterone flying around was suffocating. "Georgina and Grayson are waiting for you."

"They're safe at the castle." But she could see the hesitation in his eyes. "Look, I don't want you to be alone. With the threat out there."

"I'm a dragon," she reminded him. "If anyone tries to mess with me, I'll turn them to ash."

"I'm not talking about that kind of threat," he said, shifting in his seat uncomfortably.

"Then what—oh." When it dawned on her what he meant, she felt her cheeks go hot. "Really? You think I'm going to let some guy come in here and ravish me?" Her stupid dragon nodded its head eagerly. *Hussy.*

His eyes bulged out of his head. "He's not just any guy. He's your mate."

"So? You heard what the council said. Dragons don't always end up with their mates. Besides, Mom and Dad always said that the only thing that really sealed the deal was the actual mating bond."

"You say that but—" he cleared his throat. "This is hard for me to say because in my mind, you'll always be the little girl who used to follow us around, begging to be included in our adventures and games."

She smiled at the memory. "I'm not a little girl anymore, but I'll always be your sister."

"I know," he said, his expression softening. "And now I suppose is the time every big brother dreads."

She rolled her eyes. "Oh please, Luke. Can you really see me with that guy?"

"A couple months ago, I would have said no. But he's your mate, Sybil. You don't understand, but you will."

The word mate was starting to irritate her. In fact, the whole thing was annoying, and what he said basically echoed what she knew what everyone around her was thinking: that her mating with Aleksei was inevitable. How many times in the last few months when she saw her brothers and friends pair off, did she pray and hope for someone to sweep her off her feet? *Well, I guess you should be careful what you wish for.*

"Just, promise me you'll be the smart person I know you to be, okay?" he said, his voice resigned. "But, mate or not, I'm going to kill him if he hurts you."

That was the Luke she knew. "Not if I burn him first," she said with a wink. "Now, go to your mate and son. I'm sure they'll be wondering where you went." She leaned over and hugged him. "Take care, Luke."

"I will, Sybbie."

As she lay in bed that night, Sybil just couldn't shut her brain down. Between worrying about The Knights and then what happened at Rosie's, her mind was filled with so many questions and thoughts.

She found so many reasons why she shouldn't be mates with Aleksei, or any of the alphas. She was too young. She didn't want to leave Blackstone. So many people depended on her at work. Her family needed her.

But a small voice inside her asked, *or maybe you're scared?*

"Ha!" Her, scared? How silly. She wasn't scared of anything. Least of all, *His Royal Highness.*

Ugh, just thinking about Aleksei made her feel all kinds of things that, well, she didn't want to acknowledge. The physical attraction was there, but everything else about him—

You don't even know him.

But she didn't want to. She knew his type. Conceited. Selfish. Thinks the world revolves around them. When she was in college, she'd seen those kinds of guys on campus. Rich snobs who came from money. While those guys weren't intimidated by her family name, she couldn't stand them.

How do you know he's like them?

"I just do and—Really?" She sat up quickly. Was she having a conversation with herself? "Argh!" She punched her pillow and then threw the covers over her shoulders as she settled back in bed.

Closing her eyes tight, Sybil forced herself to go to sleep. Eventually, sleep came, though it was one of those restless slumbers where she was fully aware of her surroundings. It was when she could see light behind her lids that she knew it was morning.

Thank God. Work would be a blessed distraction. She got up and checked her phone for messages. There were some from her mom, checking in on her, and she quickly answered that. There was another one from Kate that made her mutter a curse.

Don't forget: bachelorette party tonight at The Den. Wear something white and sexy! It was followed by a series of emojis that ranged from party balloons to champagne glasses to eggplants.

Sybil groaned. She'd forgotten all about it. "I'm a terrible maid of honor and best friend." Oh well, at least Amelia—dependable and responsible Amelia—had taken care of the arrangements and the decorations.

She trudged out of bed and into the bathroom to take a shower and get ready. As she prepared her morning coffee in her to-go tumbler, she checked her schedule to make sure she had all the details. Today was another day of traveling. While it could be pretty stressful, she preferred it to staying in her cramped cubicle.

Grabbing her keys, she made her way out of her apartment. As soon as she pushed the doors open, that strange, thrilling feeling washed over her.

"Jesus!" Sybil's heart leapt out of her rib cage when she collided into something solid. She nearly toppled back, but strong arms wrapped around her.

Her dragon, of course, she knew it before her gaze landed on Aleksei.

Mine. Mate.

It was way too early for this. But she couldn't stop the warmth that spread through her belly as his grip tightened around her. She took a deep breath—a big mistake, as his scent imprinted on her senses: Aleksei smelled like a day on the beach, like ocean mist and salt and something masculine she couldn't place. Her dragon went wild, scurrying around in excitement. And then she looked up into his eyes. Her second big mistake of the morning. He stared down at her with those bright sea-colored eyes and she had to blink several times to come back to her senses.

"What are you doing here?" she asked in a voice that was supposed to come out angry, but sounded breathy instead.

"I came for you, of course." He said the same thing yesterday, but there was something different about him today, she couldn't quite figure out what. Of course, his presence was such a big distraction she couldn't think straight. They were so close, she could feel the heat of his body even through her sensible office wear.

No, she had to get her mind out of the gutter. She huffed and then pushed away from him. "What do you want *now*? Are you going to keep stalking me until I agree to be your mate? You can't do that, you're not king here."

"I came here to apologize."

Her jaw nearly dropped to the floor. In the list of "What is Aleksei going to say to me now?" *that* would have been dead last. Or it wouldn't have even been on the list at all. "E-excuse me?"

He reached out to tuck a stray lock of hair that had escaped from her ponytail behind her ear. "I'm sorry I have offended you and your family."

The touch of his calloused fingertips on her cheek was brief but sent her brain into a tizzy. At least he was wearing a shirt today. Not that it made him any less sexy. While he sported the same leather pants, he was wearing a white billowy shirt that made him look like a sexy pirate on one of those romance novels she hid under her bed. Or reminded her of Colin Firth in *Pride and Prejudice*. Plus, there was his sexy accent. She couldn't quite place it—his vocabulary was posh, but the lilt and cadence was rough. When he spoke gently and sincerely like this, it made her eardrums tingle pleasantly.

She swallowed a gulp and tried to put the maelstrom of feelings inside her in order. "You are?" she managed to squeak.

"You seemed surprised." He gave a slight cock of his head. "I was informed that my comments about your bear cousins were egregious and I regret offending you."

"Oh."

"It was not an insult, but merely a misunderstanding." He scratched his chin, a move that seemed unconscious. "Your friends informed me that you are unaware of the terms, common and fabled shifters." He quickly explained the difference between the two.

Sybil chewed on her lip. "I didn't realize that."

"Still, I have offended you, and my honor will not allow me to let such a thing pass."

Oh, it was his *honor* that made him apologize. She didn't know how to react to that, but seeing that he actually seemed remorseful made her soften toward him. "I ... if you really did make a mistake, then I suppose I could forgive you."

His shoulders relaxed. "Thank you. And I will not use that word again if it offends you."

"Well, if there's nothing else, I need to get to work." She tried to sidestep him, but he blocked her. "Yes?"

"Sybil—may I call you that?"

Again, his politeness arrested her. "Of course, A—Your ... Highness?" Maybe she should ask Christina or Catherine on how one should address royalty, since they went to a fancy boarding school in England.

"I would prefer you call me Aleksei."

That didn't seem right, but she wasn't one to question him on the use of his own name. "Aleksei," she repeated. There was something dark and heated that flashed in his eyes, but she ignored it.

He cleared his throat. "If you would permit me, I would like to get to know you better and to ... court you."

"What?" Now that really surprised her. "I mean, I ... I don't know. It's just this whole thing, you know ..." Her dragon cried in protest. "I can't."

"Oh." He seemed dejected, and her heart dropped to her stomach.

"I mean, I can't now because I'm going to work," she quickly added. "I have to travel today and check in on my clients."

"Understood," he said. "Then I will escort you as you go about your business."

"Excuse me?"

"These are dangerous times," he continued. "You are vulnerable, especially if you are traveling outside of Blackstone."

"I can take care of myself," she retorted, placing her hands on her hips.

"But what about those around you? Are you able to protect all of them, if you were to be ambushed by The Knights?"

"I—" Damn. He made a good point. What if she were visiting with one of her kids, and then someone tried to attack them? Or use them as hostages? If Blackstone hadn't come under attack, she could have brushed it off, but their enemies had struck one too many times for her to think she would be safe here. Maybe it *would* be better to use up her sick or vacation days until they figured this whole thing out. But she couldn't just take off now. "Fine."

"Is that a yes?"

"Yes." She puffed out a breath. "But, you need to stay incognito and not talk to any of my clients."

"Shall I remain Cloaked and follow you from afar?"

"What? No! I mean that's still too creepy," she said. "Look, why don't you just ride with me? You can stay in the car, if you don't mind."

"As you wish."

As he followed her to her parking spot, Sybil was still asking herself why in the world she'd invited him to come along with her. Aleksei's presence was so distracting. He was so darn big that she couldn't avoid him. When she unlocked her car and he attempted to squeeze into the passenger-side seat of her tiny Prius, it made his size even more apparent. Still, he moved with such a grace that he made it effortless, like he was getting into a limo and not her hybrid car. The vehicle dipped under his weight, but he settled in comfortably and put his seatbelt on.

She pushed the start button, then started her GPS. She already knew the route by heart, but sometimes it got lonely on her drives and it was nice to hear another somewhat-human voice. "Ready?" she asked her passenger.

"When you are," he replied.

She drove out to the next town over, Greenville. It wasn't too far away, and they were there in the town limits in fifteen minutes. The ride wasn't uncomfortable, and Aleksei seemed to be fascinated by the sights outside. She wondered how he grew up and what the Northern Isles were like. Did they have forests and trees like Blackstone? Or were they mostly rocks and seas? Maybe it was like some quaint, seaside village with huts and fishing boats. She supposed she could look it up. *Or ask Aleksei,* that voice inside her said. *You can't drive around in silence the whole day.*

It was a good thing they had arrived outside the first house before she could answer. "I'll be back." She unbuckled her seatbelt and got out of the car. The cool, crisp air hitting her face felt good. She hadn't realized how stuffy it was inside. Or maybe it was just Aleksei's presence.

This first stop was routine for her job—a welfare check for a five-year-old girl, Lucy Marks, with her new foster parents. Evelyn and Jacob Ivanko were long-time foster parents, an older couple who'd never had kids of their own, but nonetheless decided they wanted to become foster parents. Sybil had visited their mobile home lots of times in the last couple of years, and though they weren't wealthy, they provided clean beds, full meals, and as much love and care as they could for all their foster kids. The visit took thirty minutes, and while she wanted to stop and chat with Evelyn this morning, she didn't want to keep Aleksei waiting, so she said her goodbyes to the older woman and her charge, promising to come back soon.

"Hope you weren't too bored," Sybil said as she entered the car.

"I'm all right," he said. "I was speaking with Dmitri on a few matters."

"In your mind?"

He chuckled. "We are too far in distance." He held up his hand and showed her his phone.

She blushed. "Sorry, I thought … I don't know anything about that."

"Do you not speak with your father and brothers this way?" he asked.

"Not at all."

"Curious. Not all dragons can speak to each other," he explained. "Only dragons of the same type can."

"Ah, so you can talk to your dad, your brothers, and other water dragons around you?"

"Yes, the mental link is especially strong between people who are related by blood or have spent a lot of time together. I would say it's the strongest between myself and my father and we can speak over longer distances. I don't have brothers, but I have a cousin who is next in line to the throne, and we share a strong connection as well. And then there's the Dragon Guard."

"Dragon Guard?" she echoed.

"The most elite warriors in our land whose task it is to guard the royal family," he explained. "I've known most of them my whole life, and thus our connection is strong."

Sybil grew even more curious, wondering what it was like for him, growing up on an island and surrounded by a small group of friends. But, she had about another twenty minutes before her next appointment, so she had to get going. Reaching for the ignition, she stepped on the brake and pressed the start button.

"Sybil, may I ask a question?"

"Of course," she said as she pulled out of the parking space.

"This is a silly question, but what is it that you do?"

"Huh?" *Oh.* He had no idea what her job was. "Not a silly question at all." Most countries in the developing world probably didn't have access to social services. "I mean, I'm a social worker. I work for a branch of the government that provides services to people who are disadvantaged socially, economically, and sometimes physically and mentally. Though I'm mostly assigned to child welfare services, but once in a while I'll have clients who have other needs. There's just not enough of us doing this work."

"So, you care for those who are vulnerable and need the most help."

"Well, that's kind of a simple definition," she said with a chuckle.

"But it's true," he said. "In a nutshell."

"I suppose. It's mostly a lot of paperwork and going to boring meetings."

"But your work leads to people having better lives, does it not?"

"Well ..." When he put it that way, it made her work seem more noble and she didn't know what to say. Frankly, she didn't think Aleksei could be so ... eloquent. Mostly, he'd been acting like a bully, trying to get his way all the time. Today, he seemed subdued and polite. Was he sick or something?

Or maybe, this is the real him.

"Why did you want to do such work?" he asked. "Your family is wealthy, and you could have chosen any other profession."

Normally, she would have bristled at such a question, but Aleksei seemed genuinely curious. "When I was about sixteen, I still didn't know what I was going to do with my life," she said. "My brothers were going to go into business, just like Mom and Dad, and everyone assumed I would be, too. But it just didn't feel right." She shrugged. "Then one day, I don't know, I just wanted to get out of Blackstone. I mean, I've left Blackstone on vacations and I would go into Verona Mills to go out and have fun, but I've never been outside."

"I understand."

She slowed down as she reached a red light at an intersection. "I just drove around and I saw what it was like. That other places aren't like Blackstone. See, over here, we care for shifters. After all, normal humans aren't so nice to our kind." She realized she'd been living in a bubble all her life, and what she'd seen that day changed her forever. "I just thought ... well, who were caring for these people? The kids whose parents neglected them or didn't have any parents? Or the old or disabled people who couldn't rely on anyone? When I came home, I had a long talk with my dad."

"What did he say?"

"That if I wanted things to change, then I would have to be the one to take action. *Be the change you want to see in the world* ... and all that." And since that moment, she knew what she wanted to be. She could have worked for The Lennox Foundation, too, but she didn't want to just help shifters; she wanted to help everyone else.

"That is an honorable calling."

She glanced over at him, and found herself staring into the depths of his eyes again. A warmth crept up her neck. "I—"

A loud, honking sound made her start, and she realized the light had turned green. She turned away and stepped on the gas, hoping that Aleksei didn't notice the blush on her cheeks.

The rest of her morning passed by in much the same way. She had two more visits—one was a welfare check on an elderly client who lived in a remote area of the county, and another was meeting with some prospective adoptive parents. Sybil couldn't believe how patient Aleksei was, just sitting in the car the entire time. He asked more questions about her work while they drove around, and she provided the answers she could, without giving away too many details that would violate her clients' privacy.

"Are you hungry?" she asked. "We should stop for lunch."

"I am famished," he said. "Where should we eat?"

She looked at the long stretch of country road ahead of them. "I'm afraid we've slim pickings out here." She thought for a moment. "There's a greasy spoon that's popular with the locals on the way back to town," she said.

He grimaced. "A ... greasy spoon?"

She chuckled. "Not literally a greasy spoon. It's a term for a cheap place to eat. More appetizing than it sounds."

"It is American food?"

"Very American."

He paused, then nodded. "All right, I will try it."

She drove for a few miles, then turned onto the next exit. Joe's Food Hut wasn't too far from the highway, and soon she was parking her car in the lot outside the small brick building. The place was older than her and looked outdated, but both locals and visitors seemed to like it enough to keep it going.

Aleksei opened the door and she led him inside to a booth next to a window. She slid into one of the seats and motioned for him to sit across her, then picked up the menu. Sybil had been to Joe's a couple of times, and she enjoyed the all-day breakfast. She decided on the French toast and bacon, then put the menu down.

"What are you having?" she asked Aleksei.

His brows were drawn together as he perused the menu. "I ... perhaps you could recommend something?"

"What's wrong?" She couldn't hide the annoyance in her voice. Did he think he was too good for the food here? It wasn't Michelin star, but he didn't have to turn his nose up at it. "Don't you eat eggs in the Northern Isles?"

"Yes, our chef can cook eggs in many different ways." His nose wrinkled. "I'm afraid ... I'm not familiar with the food items. I know what bacon and sausage are, but what is 'chicken fried steak'?"

Shame filled Sybil as she realized how quick she was to judge. Aleksei was a foreigner, and the menu was more of a list and didn't describe each item. She could imagine how chicken fried steak could be confusing. "It's basically a beef steak that's dipped in batter and cooked like fried chicken."

"A what?" Then a lightbulb seemed to go on in his head. "Ah, I understand. That sounds ... intriguing." He looked at the menu again. "How does one exactly 'corn' beef? Is there actual corn in it?"

Sybil sighed and slid out of her side of the booth, then moved next to him. She grabbed the menu. "Corned beef is boiling beef that's been cured in brine...." She continued to explain the menu items to him, patiently answering his questions, all the while ignoring how close they were sitting together or how a tingle shot up from the bottom of her feet all the way to her stomach when her thigh touched up against his.

By the time the surly old waitress came over and asked "Whaddaya want?" Aleksei had decided on a short stack of pancakes, bacon, biscuits slathered in gravy, and home fries, in addition to the corned beef hash and chicken fried steak.

"Are you going to be able to eat all that?" she asked wryly.

"Of course," he assured her. "Aren't you hungry?"

"I am."

"Then perhaps we should order double portions."

She laughed. "Maybe we should."

In the end, she ended up taking bites from his plate. He didn't seem to mind and even placed items onto her plate without her asking. Their conversation mostly revolved around the food, and he seemed to enjoy it. His eyes lit up at every bite, and she had to admit that it was kind of cute; kind of like watching a kid discovering new things. She also never moved back to her own side, but neither of them commented on that fact.

"What do you think?" Sybil asked, not that she needed to. Aleksei had cleaned all the plates.

"It's delicious!" he declared, banging a fist on the table. "Heavenly. The mixture of salt and sweetness ... I can't describe it. It's like my brain telling me that it's exactly what I wanted."

"Better than what your fancy private chef makes?" she teased.

"I would say so." He leaned in close. "But don't tell her that."

She sucked in a breath, realizing exactly how close they were. There it was again, that mesmerizing gaze that made it hard to turn away and turned her into a puddle of mush. If he moved his head about five inches forward, their lips would be touching. The firm line of his mouth looked so inviting and she wondered how—

"Anything else I can get ya?"

Sybil jerked away from him as the gravelly voice of their waitress knocked her out of her fantasies. Her dragon whined in disappointment, and she told the darn thing to can it. "Just the check," she said quickly, then slid out of the booth. "Actually, let me meet you at the cash register."

"Sybil, let me—"

"It's fine," she said quickly, waving a hand at him. "My treat." Besides, did princes even carry cash? She was pretty sure Joe's Food Hut didn't take Amex or gold nuggets, or whatever the heck dragon princes carried around for currency.

By the time she finished paying, Aleksei was already standing by the door, holding it open. She muttered a thanks as she hurried over to her car, leaving him behind. Not that it would do any good as he caught up to her in five steps.

"Sybil!" he called, but she ignored him, instead making a beeline to the driver's side. "Wait!"

As she reached for the door, she felt him grab her arm and spin her around.

"Sybil."

He trapped her against the door, their bodies so close she could feel the heat emanating from him even though they weren't touching. "Why are you so skittish?"

"Skittish. Ha!" She hoped the laugh didn't sound forced. "I'm not afraid of you."

"I didn't say you were." He leaned down lower. "But why do you pull away from me?"

"Because—"

The ringing sound from her purse interrupting them made her sigh in relief. She ducked under his arm and grabbed her phone from her purse. "Sybil Lennox."

"Sybil, it's Angie." It was her boss. "Where are you?"

"I'm done with my morning appointments. Just finished lunch."

"Okay good, I need to you head out to Neville."

She groaned inwardly. "What's going on?"

"We just got a call from P.D. over there. Domestic violence call. A woman and a seven-year-old boy are involved." Angie's voice was calm and business-like; after all, after decades on the job, the older woman was used to these kinds of calls.

Sybil, on the other hand, was still learning. She hated these situations, and it took all her might to control herself *and* her dragon. "Emergency removal?"

"We don't know. You'll have to assess the situation."

"I'm on it. Send me the address and the details." She tapped the red button on the screen and moments later, the address popped up in her inbox.

"Sybil?" A gentle, yet strong hand landed on her shoulders. Aleksei's touch was oddly comforting, and even her dragon calmed down. "Are you all right?"

"Yeah. Just … sorry, we're not headed back to Blackstone yet. I have to make another stop."

He gave her shoulder a reassuring squeeze. "Of course, do what you must."

She drove them over to Neville County, not too far from where they were, but it was in the opposite direction of Blackstone. The GPS led them to the southeastern side of the county. This was obviously a more depressed part of town, of which she was familiar with, unfortunately. The big factory that had employed most of the people in the area had shut down nearly a decade back, and the effects were obvious. Most of the houses they had passed by were run-down or looked abandoned, almost like a ghost town. She stopped when the GPS declared they had arrived at their destination, though it wasn't hard to spot: it was the house where two police cars were waiting outside.

Aleksei eyed the cop cars. "Sybil, should I—"

"Stay here," she said in a stern voice. This was a delicate matter and the last thing she needed was a distraction. As soon as she exited the car, she headed straight for the uniformed officers.

"Sybil Lennox, Welfare Services Offices." She held up the ID hanging around her neck. "Can you tell me what happened Officer..." She glanced down at his badge. "Sarver."

"Well, ma'am," the officer began. "Dispatcher got a call from the wife, saying her husband was knocking her around. We responded and arrived here about twenty minutes ago and knocked on the door. Lady came out," he nodded toward the porch, where a man and woman were talking to two officers, "and says she made a mistake. She was angry at him for coming home drunk in the middle of the day."

"Right." Could be true, but Sybil's sixth sense was tingling. "And there's a kid?"

"That's what she said in the call, but they won't let us see him. Claims he's not home."

Something was definitely wrong. She took a deep breath. "All right, maybe I can do something." Straightening her shoulders, she marched toward the house, stepping carefully on the broken flagstone path and up the creaky steps to the porch. "Excuse me."

The officers and the couple's heads turned toward her. The woman's eyes went wide when she glanced at the ID on Sybil's chest, while contempt flickered across the man's as he assessed Sybil.

"I'm with the Welfare Services Offices," she said in her most business-like voice. "Sybil Lennox." She turned to the policemen. "Officers, where is the minor?"

"Like my wife said," the man sneered. "Charlie's at a friend's house."

"I was asking the officer," Sybil said in a cool and clipped voice.

"Look, I called your station." The woman wrung her hands together. "I said this was all a mistake. That they shouldn't send anyone over." Her voice was shaky and quiet as a mouse. Sybil's gaze swept over the woman, but she couldn't find any visible bruises. Of course, the woman was also wearing a sweater and sweat pants, and her long dark hair hung down her face. Sad to say, without any visual confirmation of abuse, there was nothing the officers could do except talk to them and try to figure out what happened.

"Mrs. Peterson, we're obligated to come and check on anyone who calls 911," one of the officers said. "It's procedure."

"I told you, Officer Reyes, we're all good, it's a misunderstandin'." Mr. Peterson's grin showed all teeth. "I had one beer on my way back from the bar and I was a little clumsy."

Sybil's nose wrinkled. While dousing himself with a bottle of cologne may have fooled the human policemen, her enhanced senses didn't miss the stench of alcohol on his breath or the bloodshot eyes. "Mr. Peterson? Greg Peterson, right? And you're Emma Peterson?"

"Yeah?" His head swung back to her. This time, his beady eyes focused and—as she was accustomed to in these types of situations—immediately focused on her chest, narrowing as if trying to imagine what she looked like underneath her blouse and suit jacket.

She mentally rolled her eyes. "If you can produce your son *and* we see that he's unharmed, we can get this straightened out."

"He's at his friend's." Greg Peterson's teeth ground together.

"Which friend? Do you have a name? Address? Phone number?" she rattled off.

"Jason or Johnson or somethin'. Sweet cheeks"—he snapped his fingers at his wife—"whatsisname? The kid with the buck teeth?"

Sybil's gaze flickered over to the window. It was dark inside, but with her shifter vision, she saw a small face peering through the window. "Charlie?" she called. "Sweetheart, are you there?" Her dragon paced inside her, anxious to know if the child was all right.

"He's not there," Peterson insisted. "Look, I know my rights. You can't enter my home unless you got a warrant or order."

Sybil ignored him, but tread carefully. "Charlie, why don't you come out and say hi?"

"Y'all need to leave, *now*." Peterson's tone was more forceful.

Officer Reyes took his dark glasses off. "Mr. Peterson, we've asked you repeatedly if your son was in the house and you've said no. If you've been lying to us, then we will have probable cause."

"Oh yeah? Maybe you'll have to speak to my lawyer." Peterson planted his feet on the floor and crossed his arms over his chest.

The knob turned and the door creaked open. Sybil saw her chance and reached her hand out. "Charlie? Why don't you come—"

"Fucking dumb piece of shit!" Greg's beefy hand shot out in front of Sybil, blocking her from the door. He must have miscalculated the distance between them because his arm hit her cheek as she stepped forward.

Something *whooshed* by behind her, the force of it making her stagger forward.

"How dare you lay a hand on my mate!" The booming

voice was unmistakable and she felt the dread growing in her stomach as she slowly turned her head.

Aleksei had his hands around Greg Peterson's neck as he pinned him to the wall. Peterson's eyes were wide with fright and his breathing was heavy. Emma Peterson let out a shriek and started screaming, while the officers stood there with stunned looks on their faces.

"Aleksei, let him go!" Sybil grabbed him by the elbow, pulling back as hard as she could. Despite her own shifter strength, she was no match for him. "Stop choking him!"

"I'm not choking him," Aleksei declared. "But I could, if you want."

"No! Just let him go!"

Aleksei growled, but released Greg Peterson's neck. "A quick death would have been too merciful for scum like you."

"Aleksei, I told you to stay in the car," she hissed.

"He assaulted me!" Peterson cried, rubbing his neck. "You saw it! You all saw it!"

"Mr. Peterson," Reyes began. "You lied to us and then you hit Miss Lennox."

"I barely grazed her!" When Aleksei scowled at him, he stepped back. "I know my rights. Arrest him!"

"Miss Lennox," Reyes said. "Who is this man? And why is he here with you?"

Shit. "He's, uh. A client. I have to, uh, bring him in for his therapy sessions." It was the only thing she could think of. What was she supposed to say? *Oh, Officer, he's actually a dragon prince from a foreign country.*

Reyes looked at Aleksei, his eyes narrowing. Dressed the way he was, Aleksei did look like he was a few sandwiches short of a picnic, and Sybil had to mentally congratulate herself on coming up with a good excuse. "Please keep him under control, Miss Lennox."

"Will do," she said, then shot Aleksei a warning glare. With all the excitement, she nearly forgot what she was here for. "Charlie, honey?" The door was now open, and a small face peered out from the crack. "It's okay, baby, you can come out. I just want to talk, okay?"

The door swung open and a small boy, about six or seven years old, slowly stepped out. Sybil knelt down to his level, her eyes trying to assess his condition. He was pale, but clean and free of marks or bruises. Of course, there were other types of wounds and scars that kid could have, non-visible to the eye. "You okay, honey?"

Brown eyes grew wide, but he nodded. "Y-y-yes."

"Can you tell me what happened?"

His mouth opened, but suddenly he closed it. "I d-d-don't know." When he looked up at his father, his slight body curled inwardly, like a plant wilting under the sun.

Sybil sent a sharp look toward Greg Peterson, who returned it with a smug smile.

"He's fine, see?" Peterson said. "Did you come home and sneak in through the back? That's probably what happened, right Charlie?"

Charlie nodded, but his lower lip trembled.

All the classic signs of emotional abuse were there, and Sybil's instinct and dragon were screaming at her to get him out of there. Unfortunately, she had to follow the laws, which always favored the parents. "Are you pressing charges, Mrs. Peterson?"

"I said it was all a mistake," she bit out.

Greg Peterson's smile turned wolfish before he said, "Get the fuck off our porch!"

There was nothing she could do. *Not now,* she told herself. The fact that the police had been called meant that the welfare office had to keep tabs on Charlie. And Sybil was going to keep an eye on the Petersons and if Greg made even one misstep, she was going to make sure he would be locked away.

"You folks stay safe," Officer Reyes said, but his tone had a veiled meaning.

"Wait, we are leaving?" Aleksei's head ping-ponged from Greg Peterson to Officer Reyes and then back to Sybil. "What about the child? It's clear that his father is intimidating him!"

"Aleksei, let's go," she said, tugging on his arm.

"But—"

"I said, let's *go.*" She flashed him a warning look.

His eyes turned stormy, but he allowed her to drag him off the Peterson property. When they got to the sidewalk, however, Aleksei strode to Reyes.

"You are an officer of the law, are you not? Sworn to uphold the law?"

"Yeah."

"Then why are you not arresting that man? He had no qualms in manhandling my mate. And that boy is obviously scared of his own father. If you could investigate—"

"We can't, Aleksei."

He turned to her with a disbelieving look on his face. "You can't?"

"It's the law."

"You can't mean that!"

"She's right, unfortunately," Reyes spat. "Without signs of abuse or a fight and Mrs. Peterson refusing to press charges, we have no probable cause to search the house or arrest him."

"I'll be writing this up," Sybil said, "and make sure our office keeps a close eye on them."

"We'll coordinate with you, Miss Lennox, if it's all right."

She handed him her card. "Call me anytime. Day or night. My personal cell is written on the back."

He tipped his hat at her. "I hope I don't have to. Have a good day now and"—he looked at Aleksei—"er, good luck. I heard therapy does wonders."

As the officers walked back to their vehicles, Sybil took one last glance at the Peterson house. Her heart was breaking for poor Charlie, and her dragon was clawing at her, telling her to go back. But there really was nothing she could do, short of breaking the law.

"This is preposterous," Aleksei said. "You can't let that child stay in that home."

"What do you want me to do?" Her voice was shaking. "Go in there and take him? That's kidnapping!"

"You are a *dragon*," he declared. "You can help that boy."

She put her hands up. "So, I'm supposed to shift and then what? Burn his father to ashes? What would that accomplish?"

"It would stop that blackguard from abusing his son and wife."

Her dragon agreed, nodding vigorously and urged Sybil to do as their mate said. *Shut up!* "Look, I don't know how things are done on the Northern Isles, but here, we don't just burn and eat people we don't like or suspect of committing a crime." She stamped her foot for emphasis. "Here, we believe in innocent until proven guilty. It sucks, yeah, but that's what prevents people from abusing the law." This was getting out of hand. She couldn't believe what he was saying and what had happened. "And didn't I tell you to stay in the car?"

"That man hurt you! I couldn't stay and let him touch you like that. You are my—"

"Shut up!" She covered her ears with her palms. "You could have gotten me fired! Good thing I told them that— er ..."

"You told them what?"

"Ugh, never mind!" She spun on her heel and stomped toward her car. Hopefully, Officer Reyes wouldn't mention Aleksei on his reports or Angie wouldn't notice when she read them.

"Sybil," Aleksei called as he strode after her.

"I have to go back to the office." She yanked the driver's door open. "Don't follow me."

"What?"

"I assume you can find your way back to your hotel? Use you magical fabled dragon GPS or something." Slipping into the seat, she slammed the door closed and then pressed the ignition button with an impatient finger. The engine had barely come to life when she slammed on the gas.

Stupid alpha dragon. What the hell was she supposed to do? She *wanted* to set Greg Peterson on fire; hell, she wanted to do that to every abusive asshole she'd met on this job. But there were rules and laws to follow. She couldn't just do what she wanted, even if she felt justified.

Of course, Aleksei had to rub salt in the wound and made her feel even more helpless and inadequate. Like she wasn't doing a good enough job, protecting Charlie and all the others.

Sybil drove for a few miles, and when her hands wouldn't stop shaking, she pulled over to the side of the road. Placing her forehead on the steering wheel, she let out a sigh.

What was she thinking, asking him to come along? She turned into an idiot around him, that's why. He just had to flash that stupidly handsome smile or overwhelm her with his large, looming presence and hot bod and she was panting like a cat in heat. And to think, she thought she was seeing a different side of him. It was an act, obviously. He probably thought she was incompetent and incapable of protecting one little boy.

Well, no more. It was even more obvious now that she and Aleksei weren't compatible and they never would be.

CHAPTER SIX

ALEKSEI WATCHED, stunned as Sybil's car disappeared in the distance. Somehow, he had driven her away. *Again.* It seemed he could do nothing right when it came to her.

In his over thirty years of existence, he had never understood women. Maybe it might take another thirty years to figure them out, but who knows if that was even possible. He was trying to help, and she just stormed off. He really didn't understand all these rules and laws. It was obvious that the young one was terrified of his father, as was the wife. If they had asked him for help, he would not have hesitated to investigate the matter further and resolved it now, before anyone got hurt.

He turned back to the house. Well, if they weren't going to do anything, he would. He Cloaked himself, blending into his surroundings so he could not be detected by the naked eye. Still, he had to be careful. He walked up the steps and opened the door slowly, then walked inside.

Peterson was sitting on a chair, watching television as he sipped from a can.

"Emma! Bring me another beer!" He let out a loud belch. "Now."

Disgusting.

The wife scurried out of the kitchen, beer can in hand, her head hung low as she quickly handed it to him.

"What the hell took you so long?" He grabbed the can from her and then smacked the side of her face with his palm. She staggered back and then hurried back into the kitchen.

Hate filled Aleksei's veins and his dragon was urging him to kill this scum *now*. And he really, really wanted to, but knew he couldn't. Even if they were back in the Northern Isles, he would still have to face trial. But, that didn't mean he couldn't do *anything*.

He waited for a few more minutes, then finally, Peterson got out of his chair and ascended the stairs. This was his chance. He followed the man as he walked down the hall and headed to the door at the end. He slipped into the bathroom just before Peterson closed it.

Fueled by rage, Aleksei revealed himself to Greg Peterson. "What the fuck!" The man started. "Where the hell did you come from? Did you break in here? I'm calling the cops!"

Aleksei grabbed his collar and slammed him against the wall. "Go ahead. What are you going to say? That I appeared out of thin air?" Calling on his dragon, he made his eyes glow with every bit of fury he felt. Scales appeared over his face and arms and he let out a fierce growl.

"Y-you're—"

He knocked Peterson so the back of his head smashed into the tile. "Your worst nightmare." He lifted Peterson up into the air. "If you ever hurt your son or wife again, I will kill you. Don't even try to run away, as I will hunt you down and tear you limb from limb. It will not be a quick death." He had to rein in his dragon, or else he really would shift right then and there. Releasing his grip on Peterson, he let the other man drop to the floor with a loud thud, then Cloaked himself and hurried out of the house. He hoped his threat was enough to deter the man, but if he knew human nature well, Greg Peterson would not be able to help himself. Some men just had the need to dominate others and take advantage of those weaker than them.

As soon as he got out, he shifted into his dragon form and leapt into the air. He needed to get out of this place, before he really lost his temper. For one thing, he was sure The Blackstone Dragon Alpha wouldn't take it too kindly if there was an incident with law enforcement and the humans.

And then he had to figure out how he would win Sybil's heart. Because, after today, he was sure of one thing: Sybil would not make a good queen. No, she would make a *great* queen. Her compassion, love of service, and her heart made her the perfect person who could rule by his side. Without the encumbrance of pesky human laws, she would be able to make a real difference in the lives of their people. They would surely come to love her.

His dragon wholeheartedly agreed. Now if only he could convince her that they were meant to be together.

Aleksei had somehow found his way back to Blackstone, though it had taken him some time. As soon as he walked into his suite, Dmitri gave him a puzzled look but didn't ask where he had been or why he and his dragon were in a foul mood. He told Dmitri that he needed some rest before the meeting with Henry Lennox tonight, and shut himself in his suite.

Finally, it was time to go and he, Dmitri, and the other members of their party headed to Blackstone Castle.

"My family and I have talked it over," Henry Lennox began, nodding to Matthew, Jason, and Luke. "While we're not convinced we should join the Dragon Alliance, we agreed that we should definitely pool our resources together so we can stop The Knights."

Aleksei watched the reactions of the other alphas and council members as they sat around the large table in the formal dining room at Blackstone Castle. For the most part, nobody had any objections, but he didn't miss the scowl on Caesar's face.

Of course, Aleksei thought to himself. Though all members of the council were equal, the Air Dragon thought himself superior to the others. He not only wanted everyone under his control, but he wanted the Blackstone Dragon's financial contribution, which was one of the requirements of having a representative in the council.

Balfour cleared his throat. "Of course, that can be discussed later."

"Good." Henry sat down on his chair. "Now, how do we start this? Do we have any information on what—"

"Wait just a minute," Caesar began. "I understand why you would have your cousins present," he nodded to James and Ben Walker, "but what are *they* doing here?" His pointed gaze went straight to the human woman and the wolf shifter seated on the Lennox side of the table.

"Excuse me?" Jason Lennox began, his voice rising. "You better watch the next words that come out of your mouth about my mate."

"I think what my colleague is wondering about is why we are including them, but not the rest of your family?" Balfour offered. "Your daughter, who is a Blackstone Dragon, is not here."

"I thought it would be best so no one gets distracted." Henry glared at Aleksei and Matthias. "She will help us if we need her. Besides, she has other important matters to attend to. But, Christina Lennox and Petros Thalassa are the representatives of The Shifter Protection Agency here in Blackstone. Christina's adoptive father, Aristotle Stavros, established The Shifter Protection Agency long ago to fight The Organization and anti-shifter groups."

"Aristotle Stavros? The Greek billionaire?" Ian asked.

"And Alpha of the Lykos Pack," Christina added. "We've been fighting these groups for decades."

"Your father has been fighting them for decades," Caesar corrected. "While we have been battling The Knights for centuries."

"Remember what I said," Jason warned.

Christina put a hand on her mate's arm. "I can fight my own battles."

Petros leaned forward and clasped his hands on the table. "It seems to me, having us here would only help our cause. Henry Lennox has already consulted with Aristotle Stavros and my alpha has pledged all his resources to stopping The Knights."

Aleksei spoke before anyone else objected. "I agree."

"I think it's a great idea," Kal added.

Ian shrugged. "It can't hurt, now can it?"

"If they already know, then there's no need to keep this a secret," Tarek said.

"I think we should just get on with it." Matthias' tone sounded bored.

"Fine, as you wish." Caesar gave his alpha a curt nod.

"Now that we've settled that," Henry said. "What's your plan for luring out The Knights and destroying them?"

Jattob, the representative of the Rock Dragons to the Dragon Council spoke up. "We wait until they strike again, and then fight them."

"Excuse me?" Matthew Lennox said. "Wait until they strike? And where exactly would they strike?"

Jason's eyes narrowed. "Here in Blackstone."

"You've made us sitting ducks," Benjamin Walker, one of the bear shifters, growled. "You want them to strike here."

"We don't *want* that," Sabir, the Dragon Council representative from the Desert Dragons said. "But if it happens, then we will strike."

"My town will not be the scene of another attack."

"We must lure them out!"

"You're putting our people in danger!"

"They're planning to strike, and this is our best chance."

The arguments and raised voices from each side grew louder, and Aleksei had just about had enough. This was one of the reasons why the Water Dragons, though part of the Council, tended to lay low and keep their participation to a minimum. Dmitri looked at him helplessly and he knew he had to act.

"Stop!" He shot to his feet, slamming his fists on the table. "Quiet down. We will not accomplish anything with arguments." He turned to Henry Lennox. "We did not conspire against you nor mean to bring danger to you and your people. But the fact of the matter is, The Knights have always evaded our grasp. We have only recently begun to fight them, and perhaps that is our mistake. We were the only ones who would have been able to stop them, and our need to stay hidden and private has made them grow strong. But it's not too late."

The tension in the room diminished and he continued. "We must work together and find a way to track The Knights, then we either strike or lure them out. Mrs. Lennox," he looked at Christina, "perhaps your Shifter Protection Agency has advanced technology that could help find them? Satellites, government databases, those kinds of things?"

The blonde woman nodded. "Yes."

"Perhaps we can start there." He gestured to the representative of the Silver Dragons. "Balfour is our Master of Information. He keeps track of anything and everything related to our history, including records of all activities and attacks by The Knights."

"I am at your service, madam," Balfour said. "Whatever information you need."

"And our dear fellow alpha, Tarek, has many spies all over the world," Matthias offered. "I'm sure he could help as well."

The Desert Dragon's cool facade broke for a moment as he scowled at Matthias. It quickly slipped back into place. "Of course. We will do our part as well."

"That's an excellent idea." Christina took out her phone. "Let me have one of our data analysts hurry here and we can begin gathering information."

Finally, we are getting somewhere, Aleksei thought. "When we find the information, then we can formulate a better plan of attack." He then looked to the Rock Dragon Alpha. "Kal is a fierce warrior and an even better strategist. He can come up with battle plans."

Kal straightened to his full height. "You will have the strength of the Rock Dragons when the time comes."

Henry Lennox flashed Aleksei a wry smile. "Well, I guess

we should all take a page from His Highness in matters of diplomacy."

But still, Aleksei couldn't help but feel proud himself, especially since it was the Blackstone Dragon himself complimenting him. "I only want victory."

"And revenge for the Ice Dragons," Matthias said in a cool voice.

They all sat down to strategize about possible ways The Knights could attack them and actions they might take in response. They theorized that Blackstone could be a possible target, but seeing as they were one of the more recent ones, it could be highly unlikely.

The evening turned out better than it had begun, and though they were far from completely trusting in each other, they were much closer to having a true alliance.

"I think we've done all we can for tonight." Henry Lennox stood up. "We should continue tomorrow."

"We can be back first thing in the morning," Balfour said.

"This is all great information." Christina hovered over the young analyst from The Agency as she typed on her laptop. "And it's all been sent to Lykos. Our people there will start looking over the notes as soon as possible."

Everyone stood up and began to leave the room. Dmitri was waiting for Aleksei outside the door to the dining room. "Your father would be proud of you if he had seen what you had done, Your Highness."

"Thank you, Dmitri. You know he always emphasized diplomacy above all else."

"Excuse me, Your Highness, may I borrow ye for a second?" Ian was standing right behind them, a mysterious grin on his face.

Dmitri bent his head in a curt bow. "Of course, Your Grace. If you'll excuse me..."

"I'll see you back at the suite, Dmitri." Aleksei's eyebrows furrowed together as he looked at Ian. "What is it?"

"Well," Ian began. "A little birdie—er, fox—told me where yer mate would be this evening."

"Sybil?"

"D'ye have any other mate?" he joked. "Of course, I meant Sybil, ye daft mon. Anyway, I was having coffee with the foxy Miss Forrester this afternoon, and she may have let it slip that the other lassies will be out tonight."

Aleksei eyed Ian suspiciously. "And why would you be helping me? Did you not say you wanted her for yourself?"

"Hells' bells, mon." Ian rolled his eyes. "Why would I want a mate when the world has so much to offer?" His wandering gaze flickered toward the only woman in the room—Christina Lennox. Sure, she was a beautiful woman, but Aleksei thought Ian would be more discreet, being that she was mated to their host, one of the few dragons in the world who could actually breathe fire.

"Seriously, Ian?"

"What?" He gave Aleksei an innocent look. "Lookin's not a crime."

"Tell that to Jason Lennox."

"Ah, dinna fash yerself over me," he laughed. "Anyway, are ye going after yer mate tonight or have ye given up?"

Give up? Was he jesting? He still wasn't sure what he had done today to offend her, but he was determined to find out and apologize if necessary. "Tell me where she is."

"It's some bar in town called The Den."

CHAPTER SEVEN

"Wow, you really went all out," Sybil exclaimed as she arrived at their designated table at The Den. A few weeks ago when they started planning this bachelorette party, Kate demanded that everything be penis-themed.

And so, Amelia, who was not only a genius at decorating but a loyal friend, did as Kate asked. The table was littered with phallus-shaped paraphernalia: dick straws inside the drinking glasses, penis-shaped paper banners around the table, little bits of glittery cock confetti strewn over and around the table, plus a ginormous sign that said "Same Penis Forever" on the wall behind them. Not only that, but everything was *pink*. It was like a penis party sponsored by Pepto-Bismol.

"You're here!" Kate declared as she pulled Sybil in for a tight hug. It was obvious that the she-wolf was smashed. Her sash that said "Holy Shit, I'm Getting Married" was falling off her shoulder and her lipstick was all smeared.

"Hey, Sybil!" Amelia greeted. The she-bear had a pair of

sunglasses that had a phallus sticking out from the scrotum-shaped lenses perched on her head.

"You made it!" Dutchy waved a penis-shaped chocolate lollipop at her.

"Of course." She planted her bag on the empty chair. "Sorry I'm late, I had a ton of work to finish. But I wouldn't miss this for the world."

"Reeeaaallly?" Kate slurred. "I thought you weren't going to come."

"Are you crazy?" Sybil exclaimed. "Hey, I know I'm always acting like a wet blanket when we go out, but tonight's special."

"Yeah?"

"Yeah! It's not every day that one of my best friends get engaged," Sybil said. "This is your night."

"You really do love me!" She looked at Sybil's outfit. "Oh, nice! I love it!"

Sybil didn't own a lot of sexy outfits, but she did find an old white lace dress she had worn to some summer party. It was long and flowy, but the sweetheart neckline showed off her cleavage. She told herself that maybe it was time to loosen up a bit.

"Wait!" Kate held up a hand, then grabbed something off the table. She placed a headband on Sybil's head. "*Now* it's perfect."

Oh God, she knew what it was. "*Kate*," she warned.

"Nuh-uh!" Kate wagged a finger at her. "It's *my* night, remember? And if I say you have to wear a dick headband, then you *wear* a dick headband."

"She's right you know." Amelia was barely able to hide her smile.

"Fine." She must have looked ridiculous, and a glance at

the window behind her confirmed it. On the headband were two plastic penises, swinging back and forth happily on springs. She groaned. "All right, I'll wear it. But someone give me a drink."

"Sybil Lennox asking for a drink? Who are you and what have you done to my friend?" Amelia joked.

"Yeah, and tell us where she is and how can we make sure she stays there?" Kate added and handed her a glass of white wine.

She wanted to ask if they had anything stronger, but took a sip. "What? I'm just relaxing." The cool liquid felt good as it went down her throat, then pooled into warmth in her belly. She really needed this right now—a good drink, the noise and being surrounded by friends. Aleksei had really done a number on her today. First, there was that almost-kiss in the restaurant, then there was the blowup after the visit to the Peterson's. The emotional rollercoaster was too much, and she just wanted to get off this ride.

"Are you okay, Sybil?" Kate asked, her expression suddenly sobering.

"Me? Yeah, I'm fine!" She downed the glass. *Oh my, that felt good.* The numbing buzz spread through her body. It wouldn't last long since her shifter metabolism burned alcohol off quickly, but she savored every second of it.

"Wow, you really do want to let loose." Dutchy grabbed the bottle of wine. "Top you off?"

"Yes, ma'am." She held out her glass and the fox shifter filled it. When Amelia and Kate flashed her concerned looks, she brushed them off. "I had a hard day at work. But this is *Kate's* party. We should be celebrating."

"We've been celebrating for three hours," Amelia said wryly.

"And the fun's not over yet!" Kate pumped a fist high in the air.

"We are not going to a strip club," Sybil protested. "I have to draw the line there. I'm going to call Petros and Mason if I even get a hint that we're seeing male strippers."

"Spoilsport." Kate stuck her tongue out. "You won't be able to reach Petros anyway. He's at that big important meeting with the alphas and council."

Oh. Right. Sybil took another sip of her wine. Her father said they didn't need everyone at that particular meeting, but he promised that he would update her on the proceedings.

It wasn't that Hank didn't want her there, he had explained, but he thought it might be best that she wasn't there to distract the alphas. While Sybil certainly wanted to take part in protecting Blackstone, she had to grudgingly agree with her father. Besides, Kate was her best friend and they had been planning this for weeks. She and Amelia also planned it on a weekday to curb their friend's enthusiasm and have work (and Cassie, in Amelia's case) as an excuse to end the party at a reasonable time.

"Well, looks like the meeting is over." Amelia turned her chin up toward the entrance.

"Why am I not surprised?" Kate said with a grin.

"What?" Sybil turned around. "Oh damn." Of course, who else would it be? She took another sip of wine and braced herself.

Aleksei and Ian walked into The Den. Despite looking out of place in their outfits—Aleksei in the same pants and shirt he was wearing today and Ian in an immaculately tailored silvery gray suit and tie—they strode across the room like they owned the place. And they were headed straight toward their table.

Mine. Mate. Her dragon cried longingly. It had been a beast the whole day, getting all worked up over Charlie and then with her leaving Aleksei. As every pair of female eyes turned to stare at them, she felt her animal roar in jealousy.

Sybil groaned and took another sip of wine. "How did they know we were here?"

"Er ..." Dutchy eyes shifted around nervously. "I *may* have told Ian."

"You told him?" Sybil's voice pitched higher.

"Wait, when?" Kate's brow lifted at the fox shifter.

"We had coffee this afternoon," Dutchy said. "What? Why are you looking at me like that? I bumped into him on Main Street and he asked me if I wanted to sit and chat. He's single and cute."

"And not your mate," Amelia pointed out.

"What, I'm not allowed to get to know men that aren't my mate?" Dutchy sipped at her wine delicately. "I've been dating since I was sixteen. Who knows if I even have a mate? Hey, it's nice that you all have met your mates, but not everyone does."

"Hello again, lovely lassies," Ian greeted. "Congratulations," he said to Kate. "Nice little hen party ye have here."

"Apologies for, uh, interrupting your festivities?" Aleksei had a confused look on his face. "Ian did not explain that you were celebrating ... something."

Sybil sighed. "Is there anything we can do for you?"

"I wanted to ... er ... speak ... uh." Aleksei's eyes wandered around as he spoke. It seemed he was determined to look anywhere but at *her*.

"Can you at least give me the respect of looking at me when you're trying to talk to me?"

He grunted. "I cannot speak to you when you are wearing *that.*"

"Huh?" She followed his gaze above her head. *Oh. Shoot.* She was still wearing the headband and the two plastic dicks bobbed back and forth, nearly hitting Aleksei in the face.

Kate guffawed, while Amelia, Dutchy, and Ian looked like they were trying not to laugh. She felt her cheeks grow hot as she ripped the headband off. "Fine."

Aleksei still looked confused, so Ian spoke up. "It's a tradition for women to celebrate their friend's last days of singlehood by giving them a party like this."

"So, to celebrate your upcoming nuptials, you get drunk and adorn yourselves with phalluses?" Aleksei looked shock.

"Something like that," Sybil mumbled.

"Perhaps we can talk in private?" he asked. "I will not take up too much of your time."

"He'll be right back with her," Ian promised. He picked up the headband and put it on his head. "There ye go, I'll try not to be a poor substitute."

Sybil supposed she could say no, but it was better to get this over with now. "All right. Let's go outside."

She didn't wait for him as she headed to the door, though she could feel his looming presence behind her. Since it was a Monday night, there weren't a lot of people around, but The Den did good business all week long seeing as it was the only bar that catered to shifters. She walked a couple of feet from the door then stopped. Crossing her arms over her chest, she pivoted to face him. "Well?"

"It seems I have offended you yet again," he said. "Was I wrong to want to protect you or the child? Is there something I'm not understanding? I'm afraid my temper got the best of me, but I'm not used to seeing such things. Back in the Northern Isles, we would never treat women and children in such a manner."

"It's not what you said or did," she huffed. "It's what you implied."

"Imply? What did I imply?"

"That … that I didn't know how to do my job!" And she had to admit, that hurt. That he thought she was incompetent when she took so much pride in her work.

"I beg your pardon?" Aleksei tipped his head to the side.

"That I wasn't doing enough to protect Charlie from his dad."

"I did not say that." He reached out to touch a finger to her cheek. "But I'm sorry my words have caused you hurt again."

She closed her eyes as his finger traced down, all the way to her chin. He tipped her head up. "Sybil, please look at me."

Slowly, she opened her eyes and stared up at his intense gaze. The sea-green of his eyes took her breath away.

"We cannot keep doing this. Me saying one thing, and you interpreting it as something else. Could you not think my intentions are good, even once?"

She saw the hurt in his eyes; real, genuine pain that made her stomach clench. It scared her, that she could see the depth of his feelings. They hardly knew each other, but all these emotions had grown so intense in the last twenty-four hours. Was this real? "Why is it so important to you that I become your mate? Is it because your family honor was hurt? What happened between our ancestors was in the past. Why can't we just leave them behind?"

His eyes turned stormy and his hands dropped to his side. "Because actions in the past sometimes leave ripples that can affect the future."

There was an undercurrent in his words that she didn't miss. "Aleksei?" There was something not quite right. "What is it? Tell me, please?"

He hesitated, but then began to speak. "When Anastasia Lennox ran away and broke the engagement, it sent our kingdom into turmoil. Those who would challenge my family's rule deemed it a weakness, a chink in our armor. Prince Haardrad's father, King Haakon, had no choice but to ask the Dragon Council to strip the Mountain Dragons of their title and lands as a show of power and strength. But it was too late." His mouth set into a grim line. "There was a civil war that lasted for a decade. Our family was able to hold back the usurpers, but not without much loss. And to this day, the broken engagement is a painful reminder of that time."

She gasped. "Aleksei, I had no idea." All her life, Sybil had thought the story of Anastasia and Silas a great big romance. It was devastating to hear that their actions had caused so much pain and that others paid a terrible price for it. "I'm sorry."

"You are not Anastasia Lennox," he said.

"I know," she said. "But still ... she shouldn't have just run away like that."

"Fated mates must fulfill their destinies," he said. "Although I cannot forget the lessons of the past, we must look to the future."

"Aleksei," she began. "Mating with me won't change what happened back then. Besides, don't you want a choice in the matter? Don't you want some say in who you spend the rest of your life with, instead of letting your dragon or fate decide?"

"I do." His gaze turned intense again. "And I have made my choice."

Sybil's knees turned weak. "This is crazy. This couldn't ..." But he didn't seem to hear her. He drew closer, tentatively placing his hands on her shoulders. When she didn't protest and instead leaned forward, his palms tracing a path down her arms, then low to encircle them around her waist, pulling her close to him. She melted against him. "Aleksei."

His name barely left her mouth when his lips pressed against hers. His mouth moved in a soft caress, teasing her lips in a way that made her feel limp. He angled his head slightly, and she sighed when his tongue licked against the seam of her mouth. Deepening the kiss, he pressed her even closer, and she could feel every firm plane of muscle in his body, including something *very hard* digging into her hip. Her body reacted, first freezing as the unfamiliar sensations of desire whorled inside her, but then settling in, wrapping around her and consuming her like wildfire.

A hand moved up her rib cage, and higher still until his palm cupped her breast. Even through the fabric of her dress she could feel the heat of his palms. She didn't stop him when he tugged down the front, releasing one breast from the dress. She moaned as a thumb found her nipple, teasing it to hardness until she was writhing against him.

"You're incredible," he whispered against her mouth. "So damn beau—"

Sybil didn't hear what he said next. In fact, she didn't hear anything at all. One moment, a loud boom was exploding in her ear and then the next she found herself on her back. Something heavy fell on top of her and she lost all the air in her lungs.

She shut her eyes tight, but the ringing in her ears wouldn't stop. The weight on top of her was gone and she felt hands all over her, checking for damage. A moan escaped her mouth as pain shot through her body when she tried to get up. Her eyes flew open. Aleksei was leaning over her, his lips moving, but all she could hear was the ringing sound. His face was full of concern. Slowly, her hearing started to come back.

"... *lyubimaya*, are you hurt? Answer me," he pleaded.

"I'm ... fine." Her throat strained and when he flinched, she realized she must have been shouting. "It's just ..." The shock seemed to wear off and she could feel the scratches on her back and arms where she hit the pavement. She flinched as she moved to fix her dress. "It's okay." She tried to push Aleksei's hands away. "Help me up, please."

Strong arms snaked under her, surprisingly gentle as he lifted her to her feet. She winced when his palms pressed against the scratches on her back.

"You are hurt."

"I'm already healing," she said. And it was true. She could feel the skin knitting together on her back. It wasn't painful, but it was a strange sensation. "Oh God, what happened?" She looked around Aleksei's large body and when she saw it, she couldn't stop the gasp from escaping her mouth.

There was a large fire in the parking lot. The flames licked skyward and even though it was dark, she could see the smoke billowing upwards was monstrous. The smell of burnt rubber and metal was acrid and she covered her nose. "What happened?"

"An explosion." Aleksei's voice was tight with tension.

People began to file out of The Den and as Aleksei turned to see the commotion, Sybil stared in horror at his back. The white shirt he was wearing was torn to shreds and the skin was bloody with deep gashes. "Oh no!" she cried. "You're hurt! We have to get you to the hospital." Her dragon roared, scratching to get out, trying to kill whoever dared to hurt what was theirs.

"It's fine. I'm already healing, *lyubimaya*." He grinned at her. "But I am flattered at your concern."

Her cheeks grew hot, and then grew even hotter at the

memory of what had happened moments before the explosion. His eyes blazed bright, as if reading her mind. Did they really— "Mmm..."

Aleksei brushed his lips against hers, quick enough that she didn't have time to protest him, but, apparently, long enough that her friends saw it. Kate, Dutchy, and Amelia stood there, staring at them with varying expressions of shock and surprise.

"Wow," Kate said in a droll tone. "No wonder there were sparks out here."

"I didn't cause this," she said defensively.

"What happened?" Amelia looked around. "Was it an accident?"

"I don't—oh no." She remembered where she parked. "My car!" She made a dash toward the explosion, ignoring Aleksei and her friends' calls. The temperature soared as she got closer, but it didn't affect her. She was fireproof, after all.

As she got to her spot, it was just as she thought. Though her Prius wasn't the vehicle that exploded, it was close enough that it turned her car into a pile of burned-out metal. "Crap."

"Sybil." She felt Aleksei's comforting presence behind her. "I'm sorry about your vehicle."

A chill ran down the backs of her legs as she continued to stare at the heap of burning smoldering steel. "I have insurance." But it wasn't the cost or inconvenience that made her spine tingle. What had set off her senses?

Sirens in the distance shook her out of her thoughts. "We should get back." She nodded to the small crowd gathering around outside The Den. "And let the authorities handle this."

The Blackstone emergency response team came out quickly. The fire department put out the flames and cordoned off the area of the explosion. Thank goodness no one was anywhere near the car that had exploded, but the EMTs were on standby, just in case. The police department, meanwhile, asked everyone to remain for interviews so they could find out what happened.

Sybil had insisted that Aleksei see the EMTs, which sounded silly now that she thought about it. He was already fully healed by the time they finished their examination, but she couldn't help it. Seeing him hurt had made her and her dragon go crazy. To his credit, Aleksei never made her feel silly, and instead allowed the EMT to examine him.

As they walked back to the front of The Den, one of the police officers stopped them. Sybil recognized him as Charlie Andrews. Charlie was a wolf shifter and was in the same year as her in high school.

"Hey, Sybil," he greeted. "Got a sec?"

"Yeah, sure, Charlie. You need to interview us, right?"

"Yeah, I heard from Kate that you were the only ones outside when it happened." He took out a pad of paper, and a pen from the front pocket of his uniform. "So, you and your, er," he glanced at Aleksei. "Friend?"

"Kind of."

Aleksei's nostrils flared. "I'm her—" Sybil elbowed him. Hard. He flinched and she sent him a glare. "We are not *just* friends."

Charlie looked uncomfortable. "Ugh, that's okay, I don't need those kinds of details." He pressed the pen to the pad. "So. Sybil Lennox. And I'll need your complete name, sir."

"Prince Aleksei of the Northern Isles, Jarl of Svalterheim,

Dragon Protector of the Eight Seas, Admiral of the Great Dragon Navy, Lord of the Barents Islands, Chieftain of—"

"Er, hold on, could you slow down, sir?" Charlie shot Sybil a look that said, *is this guy serious?*

Sybil slapped a palm to her head. "You can write down, Prince Aleksei."

"His Royal Highness, Prince Aleksei." Aleksei corrected, peering at Charlie's notepad.

"Right. And you're visiting here?"

"Yes."

"He's a guest of my dad," Sybil added. "From out of the country."

"All right." Charlie shrugged. "So, you guys were out here during the explosion? Can you tell me from the beginning what happened?"

"Well, we came out here to ... er ... talk." Sybil hoped Charlie couldn't see the redness on her cheeks. "And we were ... talking and then I heard this big boom."

"The force of the explosion knocked us down." Aleksei turned his back to show Charlie his shirt. The skin was smooth and healed, but the shirt hung like ribbons down his back.

Charlie whistled. "Whoa." He scribbled down on his notepad. "Did you see anything or hear anyone before the explosion?"

"Sorry, we weren't paying attention." Sybil coughed. "We were only out here for five minutes when it happened. Listen, Charlie." She lowered her voice. "What's going on? Do you guys know anything yet?"

"There's nothing concrete yet," Charlie said. "But ... don't tell anyone I told you this ... so the guy whose car exploded, turns out he's on the run, hiding out here in Blackstone. Not only does he have several outstanding warrants, but Chief Meacham says he's on the run from the mob or something back east."

Sybil gasped. "And they think the mob got to his car?"

"Possibly. It sounds like something they would do." But she could hear the doubt in his voice.

Aleksei's eyes narrowed. "You think there's another explanation?"

Charlie scratched his finger on his jaw. "It seems like a movie, right? I mean, guy runs away from the mob, they find him, and then plant a bomb on his car? And you know, I was a beat cop in New York for a couple years before I came back here. The real mob—like the ones who have real power—never cause such a fuss. The guy wasn't a shifter or anything, a bullet in the head would have been cleaner."

Sybil thought that made sense. But before she could ask any further, Chief Meacham, who was standing next to the burned-out car, called out to Charlie.

"Er, thanks for this." He waved his pad. "I'll keep in touch if we have any more questions. You still at the Social Welfare Office?" She nodded. "And you Mr., er, Prince?"

Aleksei snorted. "I am staying at The Blackstone Hotel."

"Great." He slipped his pad into his pocket. "I'll see you around, Sybil."

"Sybil!"

She turned around when she heard her name. Ian, Dutchy, Kate, and Amelia were walking toward them. "Did you talk to the police yet?"

"Yes." She relayed to them what Charlie had told her.

"It seems rather cut and dried if ye ask me," Ian said.

"Ugh, sorry about your car," Kate said. "I know you really loved it and saved up for it."

"Yeah." She looked back at the hunk of metal that was her Prius and sighed. The initial shock had worn off, and her chest tightened. It wasn't just the loss of the monetary value of the car that made her sad, but, as Kate said, it was one of the first things she owned that she paid for all by herself once she got her job. She bit her lip, trying to hold back the tears.

"I can give you a ride home." Kate's gaze flickered at Aleksei. "Unless, you know, you had other plans."

"What?" Embarrassment made her cringe inwardly, as she remembered what her friends had witnessed. "No! I mean, yes, I will need a ride home." *And I'll have to figure out how to get to work in the morning.* She made a mental note to send an email to her insurance agent. "But, will you give me a second?"

"Take your time." Kate gave her a wink. "I'll be over by my car."

When her friends were far enough away, she looked at Aleksei. "Uhm, so ..." She stopped when she saw the expression on his face, which was drawn into a scowl. She could feel the tension rolling off him. She couldn't quite remember why she needed to talk to him. "Are you all right?"

"I told you, I am fine." He wasn't looking at her, but rather, he looked like he was deep in thought.

"Do you have, I mean, did you drive here?"

"I flew here, of course." He was staring off into the distance, his brows drawn together.

His curtness made her step back, and the sting from his chilly tone came out of nowhere. Obviously, they had both been caught up in the moment and she had misinterpreted what happened earlier. "Great. I guess I'll see you around then." She pivoted and began to walk away. She thought she heard him call her name but ignored it and quickly jogged toward Kate.

"Everything all right?" Kate had a smug smile on her face. "I mean, you know, you two looked mighty cozy back there."

She swallowed the lump in her throat. "It's not what you think."

"Oh, yeah? What do you think *I* think?"

"I don't want to say it because knowing you, your mind's probably in the gutter." Oh God. Aleksei's lips. His hands. And the ... other parts of his body. She pushed down the desire threatening to rise up. Maybe she'd imagined it all. Why did he suddenly grow indifferent after talking to Charlie? Did he think that she and Charlie—

"Sybil?" Kate was waving a hand in front of her.

"What? I mean, can you just take me home, please?" She sighed. "I'm really tired."

Kate gave her a sympathetic look. "All right. It's been a long night."

"Yeah." *Oh no!* She'd been thinking of herself this whole time and totally forgot about Kate's party. "Sorry about your party."

Kate guffawed. "Well, I wanted it to end with a bang, right?"

CHAPTER EIGHT

ONCE SHE GOT HOME, Sybil made herself some chamomile tea before bed and got lost in a boring book about history. Usually, she indulged in some delicious romance novel before bed, but she just couldn't tonight. Not after the way Aleksei had acted. He was all over her one moment, and then dropping her like a hot potato the next. Much to her surprise, Sybil slept soundly for the most part.

It was early still, which meant she had a few minutes to get lost in her own thoughts. What exactly was going on with Aleksei? That kiss was mind-bending, to say the least. And the way he touched her ... his mouth and hands were branded into her brain.

I don't have time for this, she thought as she rolled out of bed and dragged herself to the shower. After she finished getting dressed, she trudged to the kitchen to start her coffee. If Aleksei wanted to play games, then that was his problem, not hers.

And speaking of problems, she had nearly forgotten about

her car. How was she supposed to get to work today? She had already sent a text message to Angie to tell her she might be late if she couldn't get a taxi to come out to her place. Most drivers didn't like driving to this part of town, because, well—and she hated to agree with Luke—her neighborhood *was* dodgy. She supposed she could have asked Kate or Amelia for a ride, but she hadn't thought that far ahead last night.

A knock on the door surprised her and she nearly dropped the bag of coffee beans she was preparing to grind. *Who the heck would be here this early?* It was only seven o'clock. She trudged to the door and looked out of the peephole. A man stood outside, dressed in overalls bearing the logo of a car dealership she recognized from Verona Mills. She opened the door. "Yes?"

"Miss Sybil Lennox?"

"That's me." She glanced down at the name tag on his shirt that said "Chip."

He reached into his pocket and held out a set of keys for her. "Your Prius is downstairs."

"My w-what?"

Chip checked his clipboard. "Your replacement car. My boss said I had to get this here lickety-split," he said in an annoyed tone.

She stared at the keys hanging in front of her. "Wow." She knew her insurance agent was efficient, but not *this* efficient. "Thanks."

"Sign here." He handed her a pen and she scrawled her signature on the blank line at the bottom. "It's downstairs if you want to check it out."

"Sure." She grabbed her things and then followed Chip outside. There was a shiny new Prius sitting in the driveway.

It was the newest model, as far as she could tell, while hers had been a few years old. "Am I really covered for this?"

"Don't know nothing about that, lady. I'm just here to bring it to ya. Ya got a problem with it, talk to my boss." He handed her a card. "Otherwise, I'm outta here."

Jeez, he sure was grumpy! "I'm sure it's fine." She unlocked the car and slipped inside then pushed the start button. "Whoa." Her previous car had the most basic package, but this one looked like it had all the upgrades—leather seats, GPS system built in, multimedia package, moonroof, surround sound speakers, the works. *Huh.*

She shrugged. Well, she shouldn't look a gift horse in the mouth, though this horse seems way too decked out for what she had been paying. Remembering the time, she realized that she could still make it to work early if she left now.

As Sybil drove to work, her mind drifted back to Aleksei. Where could he be now? Her dragon whined and reminded her of that soul-searing kiss last night. "Ugh!" She nearly missed her turn, and made it just in time to pull into the office parking lot. She had barely walked in when Angie came rushing at her. Angie Davenport was an older tiger shifter in her fifties with wild curly dark hair, ebony skin, and horn-rimmed glasses. She'd been the director of the social welfare office for nearly two decades.

"Sybil, we have a situation." Her boss's face was drawn into a serious expression.

"What situation?" The hairs on her arm stood on end. This did not feel right.

"It's Greg Peterson." She lowered her voice as she dragged Sybil into her office. When the door shut behind her, she motioned for her to sit down, but she declined. "All right, but don't do anything rash."

"Will you please just tell me what's going on, Angie?"

Angie sighed and took off her glasses. "Another domestic violence call to the Peterson's. This time it was a neighbor and shots were fired. Greg Peterson won't let anyone in the house and says he's got a shotgun. The police are handling—where are you going?"

Sybil was already halfway out the door. "I'm going over there!"

"I told you, the police are handling it. They don't need us yet." Angie's voice was stern.

"And when are we supposed to go there? When Greg Peterson puts a bullet in his wife's head in front of their son?" Her heart was pounding in her chest as her dragon lit up in rage.

"And what are you going to do?" Angie challenged, her eyes glowing. "When you came to work here, you told me you could control your dragon."

"I can. And I have." She tamped down the snarl in her throat. "But you know they're going to need us."

"And you have a caseload the size of Texas. What about the others who need you today?"

Sybil was torn. Angie was right; although the Social Welfare Office responded to calls like this, it wasn't usually until the end when they had the suspect in custody and the victim needed their support. If there were any victims left. She gritted her teeth. "Fine. Go ahead and fire me if you want, but I'm going there now." She had a very bad feeling about Greg Peterson, and her instinct never steered her wrong.

She breezed out of Angie's office and headed to the exit, pushing the door to head out. Her thoughts whirled around Charlie and Emma Peterson, wondering how they were right now. Somehow, she had to save them. It would be at least a thirty-minute drive to Neville, and who knows what could happen— "Holy mo—Aleksei?"

Aleksei had literally materialized in front of her, and had she been a hair faster, she would have knocked right into him. His handsome face drew into a frown when their eyes met.

"Something is wrong."

"I have to go." She pushed around him, but a hand on her arm whirled her around. "Let go, I need to be somewhere!"

"What's the matter, *lyubimaya*? Are you hurt? Did you not like the vehicle I had sent to your home this morning?"

"I'm fine and—wait, what do you mean the vehicle you sent?"

"You were in need of transportation; I got you a car. Like your old one."

"What?" Aleksei had *bought* her a car? Just like that? Jeez, did that money come from like, taxes on his people? Matthias suggested that the Water Dragons didn't have much, and from the way he dressed, Sybil had always thought that maybe they were some impoverished nation. "Why did you do that?"

"Was it not to your liking?" he asked. "I could get you something else. A ... Mercedes or a Porsche?"

"Huh? No! *Argh!* I don't have time for this." She walked away from him, toward the car *he apparently bought her* but Aleksei blocked her again.

He gripped her arms gently. "Why are you in distress?"

She blew a stray lock of hair that had somehow stuck to her forehead. "It's the Petersons. Charlie and his mom might be in danger."

As she quickly explained to him what Angie told her, his grip tightened and his jaw clenched. "I told him ..." His pupils flickered into slits and began to glow. "He will pay if something happens to the woman or child."

"Yeah, well, we gotta get there first. And it's at least a half hour drive."

"Not if we fly."

"Fly? Are you joking?" Sybil looked him straight in the eye. No, he wasn't joking. "We can't just swoop in there in dragon form."

"Why not? Shifters are not a big secret here, are they?"

"No, but Peterson's unstable. Who knows what he'll do."

Aleksei thought for a moment. "Then we will be stealthy and come up with a plan to rescue the woman and the child and have the authorities handle the rest."

This was crazy. But then again, isn't that what she had been thinking of the moment she walked out of work? Hopefully they'd get there in time. "Turn around," she said, unbuttoning her blouse.

"Why? What are you doing?"

"I'm going to shift," she said, a blush creeping onto her cheeks.

He grabbed her hand. "There is no need for that. You can ride on my back."

"Excuse me? I'm a dragon too, remember?"

"I know, *lyubimaya.*" He kissed her knuckles, a move that made her shiver. "But, you do not know the magic we use to keep our clothes on during a shift nor that of Cloaking. Would you delay us even further by changing clothes? Or give away our presence?"

"Well…"

"If you ride on my back, you will be Cloaked as well." He stepped back from her. "I will teach you the magic some other time, but for now, this is the fastest way."

Sybil didn't want to waste any more time. "Fine. But you can't shift out here."

"No one will see me. Only those I choose to see me." He stretched his arms out and began to shift. The fingers of his hands elongated and turned into those delicate fin-like wings, as the rest of his body grew and grew and his skin turned into blue-green scales. When he was done, his serpentine body was over fifty feet long, his wing span about half that. He didn't have any other limbs, so he was like a cross between a wyvern and serpent, the lower half of his body coiled around the ground and his wings flapped, sending a gush of wind. The burst of power she felt as he transformed nearly knocked her off her feet.

His head lowered and Sybil looked up into his eyes. Aleksei's sea-green eyes. He cocked his head at her, as if telling her to get on.

"This is ridiculous," she mumbled to herself. Her brothers would probably laugh at her if they found out. "Don't you dare tell anyone about this." She climbed onto his back and then hung onto one of his fins. "All right, I'm as ready as I can be."

The dragon lowered its body close to the ground and then sprang up, using its coiled tail to launch it into the air as its wings flapped. Sybil had to admit it was fascinating, how different his dragon was from hers. Her dragon's wingspan was much larger, twice its own body length which allowed it to lift off with just a beat of her wings.

Aleksei's dragon flew through the air much faster than Sybil thought he could. Maybe he was much more aerodynamic than she was, as he moved quickly. She guessed since he'd already flown from Neville, he already knew where to go and she was right. They landed right behind the Peterson's house.

She had seen the four patrol cars outside the front and her heart sank. As soon as the dragon steadied itself and began to shrink down, she slid off its back and headed straight to the back porch, not bothering to wait for Aleksei.

Sybil could hear the officers milling about outside, talking in soft voices and the crackle of the radio every now and then. She supposed they had tried everything they could to coax Greg Peterson to let his family go. She peered in through the window and used her shifter vision to see what was happening.

Greg Peterson was standing in the middle of the living room, shotgun in hand. Emma and Charlie were huddled together on the couch, and Sybil could practically feel the fear rolling off them. Emma murmured something unintelligible, which made Greg tense and stride toward his wife.

"Sybil," Aleksei whispered as he came up behind her. "Why did you not—"

"Shhh!" She held up her hand and scowled at him. When she turned back to the window, she heard a small voice cry, "No, Daddy, don't!" and then a loud, resounding slap.

Her dragon reared up inside her, then roared in fury. The heat began burning in her stomach, the dragon fire building like bile in her throat.

"Sybil..."

She could hardly hear Aleksei now as the blood rushed into her head. Her mind and her dragon melded together, and as a singular being, they walked toward the door.

She kept a tight rein on her dragon's body, but allowed it to cover her skin in gold, bullet and fireproof scales, and she pushed the door in so hard it flew open.

"Who the fuck is out there?" Peterson screamed. "I said if any of you tried to come in here, I'm going to blow—*fuck!*" Terror filled his eyes when he saw Sybil. His mouth opened again, but nothing came out.

"You scumbag!" Sybil pushed a chair that was in her way and it crashed against the wall, then splintered into pieces. He raised the shotgun at her and she laughed. "Go ahead. Try it and I'll burn you to ash."

Peterson pulled the trigger, sending the buckshot scattering toward her. She heard Aleksei's cry behind her and she spread her arms to cover him in case he was behind. The buckshot bounced off her scales, and she barely felt them. Peterson screamed as she spit a fireball at his hand, making him drop the shotgun. "You'll regret ever touching them."

The commotion outside made her freeze. Footsteps thundering across the front porch, loud male voices calling Greg Peterson's name.

"No!" Sybil felt an arm snake around her waist and pull her back. She saw the police burst in through the door as she was yanked away.

It was all too fast. One moment she was standing in the Peterson's living room, and the next she was outside, the bright sun nearly blinding her.

"Don't move," Aleksei whispered in her ear. "And don't make a sound. As long as we stay in contact, you'll be Cloaked."

Sybil froze, watching as the police officers burst through the back of the door. The two men looked around, confused looks on their faces. Despite being only six feet away, neither of them glanced their way. They looked at each other, shrugged, and then walked back into the house.

She let go of the breath she'd been holding, though her

heart continued to hammer in her chest. Her knees felt weak as adrenaline began to seep out of her.

"It's all right, *lyubimaya*," Aleksei pressed his lips to her temple. "I'll take care of you."

She felt herself being lifted up into his arms and she closed her eyes. Aleksei began to shift, and he easily perched her onto his back. Gripping his fin, she pressed herself against his serpentine body, his scales cool to the touch, but oddly soothing. They flew high in the air and minutes later, they landed.

Sybil looked up. They were in front of her apartment building. She slipped off his back and got to her feet, and Aleksei's dragon began its shift. It was still disorienting to see him fully dressed as he shrank back into human form.

"I can't believe," she said. "I ..."

He stepped forward, the expression on his face full of wonder. A finger touched her cheek and brushed back her hair. "I've never seen you more beautiful."

"You mean when I go crazy?" Was he insane? "I turned into a monster in there! I lost control and—"

"You are no monster," he interrupted. "You were magnificent. Like an avenging angel." His hand cupped her cheek. "How is it that you've seen the worst in the world, yet you remain good?"

"Good? I almost hurt someone!"

"Your control was astonishing," he continued. "You were protecting that boy and his mother. And when you're passionate about something, it's like I could feel the fire in you and your dragon. It's so blindingly beautiful and—"

She wasn't sure what possessed her to kiss him; maybe it was the remaining adrenaline in her system or maybe the sight of that shotgun pointed at her. Or maybe it was his words and the look of pure adoration on his face. No one had ever called her any of those things or looked at her that way.

His hands came down to her waist and pulled her close to his warm, hard body. She moaned, and he took the opportunity to slip his tongue inside her mouth, tasting her as she did him. He was male and musk and desire all rolled into one.

When his palms slipped lower and lifted her up, she didn't protest; in fact, she wrapped her legs around his waist, desperate to get as close to him as possible. When her core rubbed against the bulge between his legs, they both shuddered. Oh God, she wanted him bad. Wanted to see him naked and feel his skin. Would do anything to be alone with him right now.

Oh, crap.

It was broad daylight and they were in front of her apartment, rubbing against each other like cats in heat. Aleksei must have sensed her panic, and he pulled his lips away from her and let out a soft curse. He untangled her legs and placed her on the ground.

Despite her knees shaking, Sybil managed to stay upright, though she had to brace herself on him. Disappointment filled her, but she knew they shouldn't be doing this out here. Her dragon on the other hand, urged her to take them somewhere private where they could finish what they'd started.

"I'm sorry," he said. "I ... lost myself. It will not happen again."

It was like someone dumped an entire bucket of cold water on her head. Then she remembered last night, how he had suddenly pulled away from her after their kiss. *What the heck was his problem?*

"I'll try not to keep throwing myself at you," she said in the chilliest voice she could muster. She had read him wrong. Again.

"Sybil." When he reached for her, she evaded his grasp. "Don't be this way."

"Don't be *what?*" Her temper was flaring again, this time, because of him. "This is the second time that you ... you ... you stopped and ..." *Oh no.* "Is it because I'm a virgin? Is that why you don't want me?"

Something flashed in his eyes, something she couldn't name. He moved quickly, wrapping an arm around her waist and keeping her trapped. "Is this not evidence enough of my desire for you?" He pushed his erection against her, and she felt her core clench. "I did not know you were untouched." He leaned down, his breath hot on her ear. "Though it does not matter either way, the idea of being your first and last has made my desire burn for you even more."

"Then why—"

He turned her face to his and brushed his lips softly against her mouth. "Forgive me, I was distracted last night. There was something not right about that explosion."

"What do you mean?"

"I had to run back and speak with someone in the Northern Isles," he said. "A trusted advisor of sorts."

"And what did you find out?"

"Nothing yet. But as for what happened moments ago ... Sybil, you must know by now that you are much more than a romp in the sheets for me. I shall not—" His head snapped up.

"Aleksei?" She turned around. "What's—"

"No!" Aleksei pushed her down on the ground. His arms wrapped around her to cushion the impact and covered her body with his. She looked up and saw a streak of orange whiz by overhead. *What the heck was going on?*

Aleksei rolled them over. "We are Cloaked and they can't see us."

"They?" she asked. "Who are you talking about?"

"The Knights."

"They're *here*?"

"Yes," he whispered. "And they have The Wand."

That was the orange streak that passed over them. It nearly hit them, which meant ... she shuddered. If Aleksei had been a second slower ... Her dragon hissed in anger. It wanted to kill them. *No*, she told it. *We don't know how to defend ourself against it.*

He brought her up to her feet. "Let's go." He slipped an arm around her waist and dragged her to the side, pushing her up against one of the columns that supported the roof of the driveway. They stood still, waiting.

Five men walked toward them, all wearing similar wine-colored robes. One of them held something long, like a staff. It was made of a dark-colored wood and had an orange jewel on the tip. Sybil shivered. Aleksei didn't have to tell her what that was.

"Where are they?" one of them asked.

"They must have run away," another answered.

"You fools!" the third one yelled. He was the one holding the wand. "Dragons can turn invisible!"

"But not her!"

"The other one was with her. We know the others can turn invisible. Did no one bring the heat goggles?" The others looked at each other. "Idiots! You're all incompetent idiots. First you accidentally detonated the bomb too soon, and now this!"

The first man held his hands up. "Hey, I'm not trained in setting off bombs. Jake said it was easy, that all I had to do was plant the thing at most three cars away and once she got in her car, press the button. But it just went off."

"It would have been a poetic death," the third man cackled. "Her dragon taken away, the bitch left vulnerable, and then being burned to death."

His words made Sybil's blood freeze in her veins. They were talking about her. Aleksei's body tensed, but he didn't move.

"Janus, what do we do now? Lord Harken will be displeased we failed in destroying the unmated female."

"He will be, for sure, but it is what it is," Janus replied. He slipped The Wand back into his robe. "We will report back to Lord Harken and see what he wants us to do." The five men looked around one last time, then walked toward the road. There was a roar of an engine, then silence. They waited for a few seconds, then Aleksei stepped away from her.

"I will destroy them all," he said in a low, menacing voice. "They dare try to kill my mate? They will not live to see—"

"Aleksei!" Truth be told, she was scared—of that murderous look in his eyes. She could feel the fury of the dragon inside him, like a tightly-contained storm inside a bottle, ready to burst. It pained her to see him like this. "Please. Calm down. I'm here." She touched his chin and tipped it down to meet her eyes. "I'm safe. Here. With you."

"Sybil, if something happened ..." He cleared his throat. "I must ensure your safety."

She didn't know what to say to reassure him. She had heard it with her own ears. The Knights were targeting her. They knew where she lived and about her dragon's capabilities. "Maybe they'll give up."

"They won't," he said firmly. "We must speak with your

father. We will head to the castle at once. Perhaps you should contact one of your brothers."

Sybil didn't have the strength to fight. "Fine. I'll call Kate." Kate would be at The Agency headquarters and would have a more even head about this whole thing. She could only imagine how Matthew, Jason or *Luke* would react if they found out what happened.

CHAPTER NINE

"I'm going to fucking end them all." Hank Lennox's eyes burned with the heat of the fire that his dragon kept inside him.

"My thoughts exactly," Aleksei said, though he didn't quite put it in such crude words. He was a prince, after all. His dragon, on the other hand … well, if it could talk, it would probably make everyone in the room blush.

"First, we need to keep you safe," Hank said to Sybil. "You're going to stay here from now on."

Sybil was seated on the sofa in Hank's private study, next to her mother. Riva had an arm around her daughter, barely able to keep from breaking down when she heard what happened. "Dad!" she protested. "I'm not going to be a prisoner here."

"Dad's right," Luke Lennox added, crossing his arms over his chest. "You need to stay where we can keep an eye on you."

"I'm an adult, I can take care of myself." She crossed her arms over her chest in a petulant manner.

"Well, you sure aren't acting like one," Jason Lennox shot back. "Jesus, Sybil! We almost lost you. Twice, apparently."

"You're all overreacting," she said.

Aleksei shook his head mentally. His mate was a stubborn one.

"Overreacting?" Matthew echoed. "You almost died and they're still trying to kill you! We're *not* overreacting."

"Darling," Riva's voice was soothing and calm. "Would it be so bad? You can stay in your old room, and we can hang out. Meg would be thrilled to have you."

"That's exactly it!" Sybil shot to her feet. "I'm a sitting duck now. What if they try to attack the castle? What about Mom?" She looked at Hank, then turned to her brother. "Or Catherine and the baby? What about Meg and Christopher and the rest of the staff?"

"We'll hire guards," Hank said. "Twenty-four hour protection. And I'll be here too."

"You're all being ridiculous."

The Lennoxes continued to argue amongst themselves, and Aleksei could do nothing else but watch them. He could see both sides, of course—he wanted to protect Sybil, but at the same time, everyone around them would be vulnerable. Anyone around her could be in danger, now that they knew The Knights wanted her dead.

Aleksei had time to think of all of this. Indeed, last night, after the explosion, he had called home, to one of the most trusted members of the Dragon Guard and the smartest scholar he knew. Gideon had been gathering intelligence about the Wand and The Knights ever since the attack on the Ice Dragons.

No one knew what it looked like exactly or how it worked, but Gideon had found an ancient etching of the Wand. He sent it to Aleksei and it was definitely the weapon he saw today.

Gideon had even more alarming news: according to their sources, The Knights looked like they were gathering, not just in one place, but in pockets. The Middle East. Europe. The British Isles. And yes, even America. The vacuum left by the death of The Chief had definitely been filled and they were getting ready to strike. Perhaps it was this Lord Harken the men today had spoken of. He'd already sent the name to Gideon in hopes of finding more information.

The din in the room was getting louder. His mate's face was red and he feared that all four Blackstone Dragons would make an appearance. And so, he held up his hand. "Excuse me!" All eyes turned to him. He cleared his throat. "I may have a solution."

"You do?" Sybil asked.

"Yes." All right, it wasn't a solution, but he knew it was the only way. "I will protect Sybil. In the Northern Isles."

"Excuse me?" Sybil's voice increased in pitch. "I'm not going anywhere with you!"

"She stays here," Luke groused. "Where her family can protect her."

"How will that help?" Matthew asked.

"We don't even know where that is!" Jason protested. "If we're sending her away, then she should go to Lykos."

Aleksei would never agree to that; he wouldn't trust wolves to guard *his* mate after all. He was about to object when Riva spoke up.

"I think it's a great idea."

Now all eyes turned to the lone human female. Even Aleksei was flabbergasted.

"Darling," Hank began, but she waved a hand at him.

"No one knows where the Northern Isles are located exactly, correct?" Riva said.

How she figured that out, Aleksei didn't know. "No, madame. The islands are protected by magic and its exact location is not on any map."

"Not even The Knights?"

"No, madame. Only its inhabitants know and we are all sworn to secrecy. For our own protection."

"Then it's perfect." As the men began to protest, she stood up and put her hands on her hips. "Which one of you would *not* lay their lives down for *their* mates?" Silence greeted her. "Then you all agree where Sybil would be the *safest*." She turned to Aleksei. "Your Highness, I trust that you will take care of my only daughter?"

Aleksei had only felt scared a handful of times in his life. But, looking into the serious depths of Riva Lennox's brown eyes, he suddenly had an inkling of what real fear was like. Even his own dragon was stunned into silence. "With my life. I swear to you, madame, there will be no place safer."

She looked smugly at her husband and sons. "Then it's settled. Come on, darling," she tugged at Sybil, who was still standing there with her mouth open. "Let's go pack."

And just like that, Prince Aleksei of the Northern Isles had found the greatest ally of his life in the form of a tiny human woman. He just hoped he could keep Riva Lennox as an ally, as he surely wouldn't want her for an enemy.

CHAPTER TEN

"You don't seriously think this is a good idea, do you, Mom?" Sybil was staring down at her mother, who was kneeling by the closet.

"There! I found your overnighter." Riva held up the bag in triumph then looked back at the closet. "I'll ask Christopher to bring in my suitcases as well. What's the weather like in the Northern Isles, do you think? Should you be bringing sweaters or shorts?"

Sybil groaned, then threw herself on the double bed. Her room at Blackstone Castle hadn't changed much from when she left before going off to college, and the staff and her mom had kept it clean and neat all these years. Sybil mostly used it to store her off-season clothes and her knickknacks from growing up. A poster from the first concert she ever attended still hung on the wall.

"They probably don't have guidebooks for the Northern Isles, do they?" Riva asked nonchalantly.

Sybil looked up from where she lay down. "I doubt secret islands that have magical protection do, Mom."

Riva frowned, dropped the sweater she was looking at, and then walked over to her daughter. "Darling, what's the matter?" She dragged Sybil upright. "Is this like that time you didn't want to go on that camping trip with Kate and Amelia?"

"I think this is a little bit different than that," she said sarcastically. "I can't believe you're agreeing to this. Have you gone mad, Mom? Why would you want me to leave?"

"I don't want you to leave, sweetie," Riva said. "I want you to be *safe*. When you told me what happened, I was beside myself." Her breath hitched. "I don't want anything bad to happen to you." She took a deep calming breath.

"I know, Mom." She hugged Riva. "I just can't believe you're okay with me going with Aleksei."

"Darling, he's your mate. He'd sooner die than let you get hurt. Now, tell me: what's *really* the matter?"

Her mother's words rang in her ear. "I don't ... I just didn't think it would be this way, you know? Aleksei is just so ... he's too much."

"Are you frightened, darling?"

She bit her bottom lip. "I don't even know why the whole thing scares me. This is supposed to be easy for shifters, right? That the universe decides for us and we don't have to worry about it. But, it's all so ... so big, and sometimes I feel like I'm being swallowed whole. And I'm afraid that when it's all said and done there won't be anything left of me."

"Oh darling, if there's something I've learned, love and relationships are never easy, mates or not." Riva took a deep sigh. "I need to tell you something. Something about me and your father that no one knows. Well, no one except Uncle James and Aunt Laura."

"What is it?"

"Well ..." Riva hesitated, but continued. "Most people

assumed your father and I started dating because he had business with Sinclair Construction. That's partly true." She paused, then straightened her shoulders. "Our marriage was part of an arrangement. Your father bailed the company out when we were in trouble and in turn I had to marry him to produce an heir. I didn't meet him until our wedding day."

Sybil was so taken aback she shot to her feet. "What? Why didn't you tell us? Was it a secret? What ..." Oh God, was everything she knew a lie?

"Sybil, please sit down. We didn't mean to keep this from you or your brothers. None of you asked, after all. And it just wasn't important anymore."

"Not important?" Sybil voice raised. "Dad ... he really is your mate, right?"

Riva laughed. "Of course, he is. I didn't understand it myself since I'm human. But he said, the moment he saw me, he knew. Or his dragon knew, though he was denying it for a while. But, we couldn't stop it. We fell in love along the way."

Sybil stared at her mother, speechless. "Why are you telling me this now?"

Riva took her hand and pulled her down to sit next to her. "Darling, if you don't want Aleksei or if he does something to hurt you, you just call me and I'll do whatever it takes to bring you back home."

Sybil had no doubt her mother was serious.

Riva continued, "But, I hope you keep yourself open to the possibilities. I can't even begin to tell you what it's like, to have a mate and experience love together. It feels big and scary, yes. But I promise you, if Aleksei is even half the man your father is, you'll come out of it whole. He won't let you be swallowed up."

Sybil bit the inside of her cheek. "But, I've only known him for a few days."

"I know it's quick, but it's not about how fast you fall."

There was another thing that was bothering her. "Mom, I haven't ... I mean, I've never ... I haven't ... been with anyone. Ever." Her face felt like it was on fire. She couldn't believe she was telling her mom this.

Riva must have sensed what she was trying to say, as her face lit up. "Oh. Darling, it's all right. Don't be embarrassed. Sex is a beautiful thing, especially with your mate."

Sybil wanted the earth to swallow her up. *At least Dad wasn't here.* "I know the mechanics. But what if I do something wrong?"

"Darling, just do what feels right. Aleksei knows, right?"

She nodded. "And we've uhm, kissed. And stuff."

"How was it?" Riva asked in a teasing voice. "Is he a good kisser?"

"Mom!"

Riva chuckled. "I don't know him very well, but he's your mate and I've seen how he looks at you."

She frowned. "How do you mean?"

"He wants you. But also like you're the most precious thing in the world. As if no one else was in the room when you're around. Why do you think I want you to go with him?"

Sybil sucked in a breath. "All right. I'll keep myself open to the possibilities. But what if it turns out we want different things?"

"Then, my darling," Riva began with a smile. "You negotiate."

"Negotiate?"

"Men call it compromise, but you're my daughter and we negotiate." Riva winked at her.

"Everything okay in here?"

Sybil and Riva both looked up. Hank was standing in the doorway.

"You guys are taking a long time," he said. "Anything I should know about?"

Well, Mom thinks I should lose my virginity on this trip so ... "Sorry, we just couldn't decide what I should bring."

"Aleksei is arranging transportation now," Hank said. "You should be able to leave this afternoon."

"Darling, why don't I go ahead and pack for you?" Riva said. "You go and spend some time with your dad and your brothers. I'll have Meg make you a batch of her chocolate chip cookies."

"She's not going away to camp." Hank's brows were furrowed together and it was obvious he was not happy with the arrangements, but had no choice.

"Shoo!" Riva waved them away. "Just go, okay? I'll join you as soon as I'm done."

Hank sighed. "C'mon, Sybil, let's leave your mom alone. She's obviously making plans." He muttered something about "weddings" and "over my dead body" under his breath, but Sybil didn't quite hear all of it. When she looked back before she left, she saw her mother's expression and she groaned. Riva was definitely planning something.

A few hours later, Sybil and Aleksei were on their way, with Luke driving them in his truck. Hank and her brothers had stayed behind as they were about to meet with the other alphas. They, along with Aleksei, had agreed it might be best to wait until Sybil was gone from Blackstone before they told the other alphas and the council what had happened.

"They won't be happy about it," Aleksei had warned.

"Do you care?" Hank had asked.

"Not really," Aleksei said smugly. "The Dragon Council is a necessary burden, but I owe them no loyalty."

Sybil sat in the back of the truck, watching the scenery go by. It had all been so fast, and she wasn't even sure where they were going. At first, she thought they would be shifting and flying together, but that wasn't exactly safe. Besides, Aleksei said they would have to fly or swim for at least eight hours straight, and while he could do that portion of the trip, Sybil wasn't used to being in dragon form that long.

So, where the heck are we going?

"We're here," Luke announced in a gruff voice.

Sybil looked outside. "And here is ...?"

"A private air strip," her brother said, as if that explained everything.

"Private ..." She peered out the window. A jet was standing on the tarmac. "Aleksei, you didn't have to rent a private jet. We could have flown commercial."

"There are no flights to the Northern Isles." He slipped out of the front passenger-side seat, and then opened her door. He helped her out of the truck. "And I didn't have to rent a jet."

"You didn't?"

"No." He nodded his head at the plane. "This is my private plane."

"Your ... what?" She turned toward the jet. Up close, it was much larger than she had thought; even larger than the Lennox jet, which she'd only flown in a handful of times. The plane was white, sleek and shiny, and bore a large gold emblem on the front. "You ... your ... you own a plane?"

"Well, the Royal Family of the Northern Isles does," he said. "This is one of three planes we own, and the one I usually take."

"Wait. A. Minute." Her jaw practically dropped to the ground. "You're *rich*?"

"I never said we were poor," he said nonchalantly. "Anyway, does it matter? You too are the daughter of one of the wealthiest men in the world."

"I ... I mean, I suppose it doesn't matter." Oh dear. What had she gotten herself into?

"Ahem." Luke was standing beside them, an inscrutable look on his face. "Everything okay, Sybbie?"

"Yeah." She stepped forward and Luke opened his arms, drawing her in for a hug.

"It's not too late," Luke whispered in her ear. "You know I'll protect you if you stay here."

Her throat tightened. "I don't doubt that. But I'm doing this to protect *you*. And Georgina and Grayson and everyone." She had a target on her back and The Knights had already proven that they didn't care who got hurt in their pursuit of her.

He huffed. "I don't like the idea of you being in a foreign place by yourself."

"I'll be fine," Sybil assured him. "We'll take down The Knights and then I'll be back."

"Of course." But Luke's didn't sound confident in his own words. In fact, now that she was staring at his face, he looked almost wistful.

"I'll see you soon, Luke."

"See you, Sybbie." He gave her one last hug. "You better take care of her," he warned Aleksei. "And treat her right."

"I shall treat her with the utmost respect," Aleksei vowed. "Thank you for trusting her with me."

"I *don't* trust you," Luke said. "But I know you'll keep her safe." He turned and began to walk back to his truck.

Aleksei steered her toward the stairs, placing a hand on her lower back. Her heart began to pound, realizing that she would be alone with him for the next few hours. Her dragon, on the other hand, seemed to relish it, as if saying, *finally*. It was encouraging her to kiss him again as soon as the door to the jet closed.

Ninny, she told it. *There's going to be other people in there.*

He guided her up the stairs and into the jet, where a tall, handsome man was waiting for them, his back ramrod straight. The man was dressed in an immaculate white uniform suit that had the same gold emblem over the pocket of his jacket that was on the side of the plane.

"Your Highness, Miss Lennox. Welcome aboard." He gave a deep bow. "My name is Oskar, I'll be your steward for the flight. It is my pleasure to serve you."

"Thank you, Oskar."

"Please, come this way."

Sybil had hoped she could contain the shocked expression on her face, but she doubted that now. She couldn't help but look around. If she thought the outside was impressive, then the inside was even more opulent, though very tasteful. There were six leather seats in the front, and behind them was a couch and two love seats. A set of stairs were installed in the back, probably to the private bedroom. And everything looked lavish, done in white and gold with touches of blue-green. As she sat down on the first chair on the right side, she nearly groaned at how buttery soft the leather felt. She glanced over at Aleksei, who, despite being dressed in his usual worn leather pants and white shirt, looked absolutely comfortable in his surroundings. In fact, he seemed almost downright bored, while she probably looked like a country bumpkin on her first trip to the city.

"Are you all right?"

"I'm sorry, I just can't get over … I mean. You swam and flew all the way to Colorado! Why didn't you just take your jet here?"

He sighed. "Well, first of all, all the alphas agreed it would be best to come in without being detected. It was necessary for safety, in case The Knights were monitoring our movements using our passports or scanning passenger manifests on planes."

"Oh." That made sense. She already knew that the influence of The Organization was far reaching. "But why hide that your country is prosperous?"

"The Water Dragons have always preferred to keep our wealth a secret. That way, no one will bother us. Ever since the kingdom was established hundreds of years ago, secrecy has always been the best way to ward off invaders and others who would harm us. We are self-sufficient and do not need to trade with others, which has made it easy for most large countries to ignore us. Most people who do know about us think we're some backwater country with limited resources and we just don't bother to correct them."

"I see." She could understand that. After all, she and her family were private people as well.

"I apologize if you felt you were deceived," he said. "It was a necessary ploy."

She smirked at him. "And now that I know your secret, am I going to have to 'sleep with the fishes?'"

He laughed. "I have always enjoyed *The Godfather*. I thought Marlon Brando was a great actor. My American roommate at Oxford showed it to me one night after we'd finished studying for finals."

Her jaw dropped. "You went to Oxford?!" What other secrets did Aleksei hide? She wasn't sure she was ready to find out.

CHAPTER ELEVEN

As Aleksei sat on the plush leather seat in the front of the plane, his thoughts turned to what would be awaiting him back in the Northern Isles. There was much work to be done and he knew that everyone would have a lot of questions about his trip and the progress with The Knights. Still, it would be good to be home. Even though he had only been gone a few days, it felt like forever. So many things had happened since the time he left, after all.

He had spoken only briefly to his father, and explained the situation. King Harald had been surprised, and of course when he learned his son and only heir's mate was in danger, he immediately gave his permission for her to come. In any case, the jet was actually already on standby, ready to whisk Aleksei away should the need arise. His father was also excited at the prospect of meeting Sybil.

"Your mate? You are certain, my boy?" King Harald had said.

"Absolutely, Father."

"This is ... exciting news indeed. Although I wish it had

been under better circumstances. But tell me, what is she like?"

He wished he had the time to tell his father about Sybil. It would have taken hours, but instead he simply said, "She's perfect."

"I cannot wait to meet her then." King Harald sounded positively giddy. Aleksei was sure he was already planning a royal wedding and having the nurseries cleaned and redecorated. After all, Sybil being a dragon meant that dragon children were a guarantee, and being mates meant that the chances of having children would be even higher. Of course, he knew that possibility was not far off, though there were other things he had to do first. Mainly, get Sybil's consent.

"Your Highness?" Oskar said in a polite tone. "We are almost home. Shall I fetch Miss Lennox?"

"No." He stood up. "I shall go."

He walked toward the guest bedroom, which was located just under his. Having Sybil so close, yet unable to be with her was torture. His dragon urged him to make her theirs, but he had to control himself.

Knowing that she was a virgin had changed things. Not his feelings for her, which only grew stronger each day. No, he knew he had to handle her with care, and not just physically. He wanted *her* to be sure, because once he made love to her, there would be no one else—for either of them.

Clearing his throat, he knocked softly on the door. "Sybil. Are you awake? We are about to land."

There was movement inside the room, then a few seconds later, the door opened. Sybil stood in front of him, wearing a long gray sweater, dark trousers, and boots. Her hair was swept to one side and her face wore only the barest of makeup. "You look lovely," he said. His voice was controlled, despite the desire threatening to spill over as his eyes roamed over the curves of her generous breasts straining against the sweater. What he wouldn't do to push her down on the bed behind her and have his way with her.

"Thank you." A blush crept into her cheeks. "I wasn't sure what would be appropriate to wear. I hope this is okay."

"It's fine." It was more than fine, and he felt an unreasonable surge of jealousy, knowing other men might be looking at her. "No one knows we are arriving and there won't be any formalities. And, you won't be meeting the king until later. We'll be dining with him and a few guests tonight."

"Oh." Her eyes grew wide. "I didn't bring ... I mean, I'm not sure I have anything to wear to any formal gatherings."

He cursed to himself. He hadn't thought of that. "Do not fret, as I will have someone assist you. Ursula will be able to find you something."

"Ursula?"

"She was my mother's personal lady-in-waiting. She stayed on to run the palace after my mother's death."

"I didn't know. About your mother. I'm sorry."

He looked at her somberly. "It's quite all right." It had been a decade since she passed. Still, the pain of her death hadn't lessened. "She would have liked you."

"Oh? Tell me more. If you don't mind."

"If you wish, but," he offered his arm. "We are nearly there. We should take our seats."

"Right." She slipped her arm into his and allowed him to lead her to the front of the plane. "So, your mother ... did she grow up in the Northern Isles?"

As Sybil sat down, he took the chair next to hers. "Actually, no. She was a princess from a small, but now-defunct country in the Baltic region. She doesn't remember much about it, as she and her family always lived in exile."

"How did she and your father meet?"

"It was an arranged marriage." He frowned when he saw Sybil's eyes shift and the pulse in her delicate neck jump. "Don't worry. She and my father grew to love each other. He never did remarry after her death, claiming that my mother was the love of his life."

"Sounds romantic." Her eyes lowered and another blush deepened the color in her cheeks.

Sensing her discomfort, he tipped her chin up with his finger. "What's the matter, *lyubimaya*?"

"I just ... I was thinking ... everyone will know who I am. That I'm related to Anastasia Lennox." She shifted in her seat uncomfortably. "The war ... they might not like me."

Aleksei had never thought of this possibility. "Only fools would not see what a good person you are. As you said, that was the past. There may be some traditionalists who might not take it kindly that you are here, but they will have to get over it." Sybil was going to be his wife and their queen, after all. "But, for safety's sake, my father and I have agreed it would be best not to tell anyone who you are. Only my father and the Dragon Guard know your true identity."

She seemed relieved. "Thank you."

"Your Highness, Miss Lennox," Oskar said. "I will be taking my seat for our landing. Please do put your seatbelts on."

"Allow me." He reached over her, strapping the seatbelt across her lap, though really, it was an excuse to get close. He longed to take her in his arms and kiss her again, but for now he was content to be just close enough to smell her scent. His dragon growled and he snapped back to reality. It was getting harder and harder to control his animal, and surely, if any other dragon noticed how it was when Sybil was around, they might suspect something. He had to rein himself in.

As the plane made its descent, Aleksei braced himself as the plane shook and the lights dimmed for just a second before they flickered back on. Sybil quickly grasped his hand, threading her fingers through his.

"It's all right, *lyubimaya*." He gave her hand a squeeze. "We are passing through the magical veil that protects the Northern Isles. Look outside and you'll see it now."

Sybil peered outside the window, then gasped. "Is that it? The Northern Isles?" She pressed her nose against the glass. "It's so big! How did you manage to hide it all?"

"It's not that large," he said. "The main island you're seeing is no bigger than Luxembourg. Twelve other smaller islands surrounding it are probably the size of Hawaii." He scratched his head. "We're actually not sure how the magic works. See, the cloak that hides us from the rest of the world had already been here when my ancestors came. For some reason, we Water Dragons are able to see through it. As far as I know, no other dragons, shifters, or humans can, at least no one has tried."

"What are those red things all over the place? They look like mini oil rigs."

"Wave generators," he explained. "We have them to create power, as well as wind turbines and solar panels, plus some geothermal plants. The entire country is powered by one hundred percent renewable energy."

"That's amazing."

"We started using renewable resources about twenty years before the rest of the world, mostly out of necessity."

The plane dipped lower and soon, the wheels touched the

ground. The landing was smooth and the plane slowed down the runaway until they eventually came to a halt.

"So, where are we exactly?" she asked. "Or can you give me an estimate?"

"We are in the center of the Norwegian Sea, right in the middle of Iceland, Svalbard, and Scandinavia. But to be more precise"—he clicked his seatbelt off—"we are on the private airstrip of the Royal Family of the Northern Isles, just outside the capital city of Odelia."

Sybil unbuckled her own seatbelt. "What's going to happen now?"

"We will be heading to Helgeskar Palace. First, I must speak to my father." He offered her a hand and helped her up but didn't let go. "One of the Dragon Guard should already be here to fetch us. Oskar," he turned to the steward, who had magically appeared behind them.

"I shall make sure Miss Lennox's things arrive at the palace promptly, Your Highness." He gave a deep bow, then walked toward the front of the plane. Turning the big lever on the door, he opened it, the air rushing in making a loud *whoosh* sound.

"Thank you," he said. "Come, *lyubimaya*."

They walked hand in hand. The steps were already waiting for them and they descended to the tarmac. There was a dark-colored SUV with blackout windows by the foot of the stairs and a large man was standing there, his arms stiff at his side, his back ramrod straight, and a serious expression on his face. His hair was midnight black, shaved on the sides, though he sported a long, thick braid that went down his back. Eyes like steel clashed against his and he made a deep bow.

Welcome home, Your Highness, Stein said through their mental link.

Thank you, Stein. Do you mind speaking out loud for the time being? She's not used to mind speak and I want to put her at ease.

Of course. "Your Highness, welcome back." His voice was gravelly and rough.

"Thank you, Stein," he said. His gaze flickered at Sybil then back to the other man. "I trust Thoralf has explained to you who our visitor is?"

"Yes, Your Highness." He didn't elaborate or say anything more, but that didn't surprise Aleksei. Stein was a man of few words, after all.

"All right, let's go to the castle then."

Stein opened the door for them and Aleksei helped Sybil inside the SUV. She scooted over and he climbed inside, but made sure to keep some space between them.

Sybil stared out the window as they drove out of the airstrip. The thick forest surrounding the airstrip soon turned into an expansive highway and they turned onto the exit that would lead them into the capital city. He watched in fascination as Sybil's gaze seemed to drink in the sights.

"It's like Europe, but more modern," she said.

"We've kept most of the old buildings," Aleksei said. "It has that certain charm of the continent. But, we've modernized the roads and imported electric vehicles as well."

"No wonder the air smells really clean."

It didn't take them long to reach the palace. They drove through the gates and to the private garage in the back. The staff had been cleared and ordered to stay away from his wing of the palace, unless they were summoned. Stein stepped out and opened the door for them.

"Now," Aleksei began as he helped Sybil out of the SUV. "Someone will show you to your rooms while I meet with the rest of the Dragon Guard to plan your security detail."

Sybil frowned. "Don't you think I should be part of that meeting?"

"Do not fret. I will take care of you."

Her eyes narrowed. "Aleksei, I'm sick and tired of being dragged around like some rag doll. I've already left my home, and now I'm in a strange place and I feel like I've lost control of my own life. For once, I'd like it if I wasn't treated like some child. I'm a dragon too, remember?"

He smiled fondly at her. "Of course, how can I forget." The fire in his mate hadn't diminished. In truth, he'd been worried throughout the whole flight. She seemed nervous and unsure of herself. "Fine then." He looked at Stein. "Make sure everyone is gathered in my office. Miss Lennox and I will be waiting."

Stein's face remained impassive. "Are you sure that's wise, Your Highness?"

Sybil's eyebrows just about hit her hairline, but Aleksei placed a gentle hand on her elbow. "Are you questioning me, Stein?"

That made the gigantic man swallow hard. "Of course not, Your Highness. As you wish." He made a deep bow. "Excuse me."

"Let's head inside."

Aleksei hoped she was ready to meet the Dragon Guard of the Northern Isles. They were the fiercest warriors in the country, but they were also his closest friends. In front of other people, they followed strict protocol and treated him like a prince, but in private, they all jested like boys. Hopefully, his mate could be strong enough to stand up to them.

Aleksei sat in his chair behind the large oak desk and he looked up to watch Sybil as she stood by the window. The sunlight streaming in from the window made her appear ethereal, and he found himself unable to turn away. He could watch her all day.

Mine. Mate.

His desire to make her his was growing the more time they spent in each other's company. If he didn't have her soon …

No.

He vowed to do the right thing, and the only time he would be with her was when she was ready to give him everything, because he would not settle for anything less. Because if anything, she already owned all of him.

"Ahem."

The discrete cough made him turn his head. "Thoralf," he called to the captain of the Dragon Guard. "Come in." He saw the figures looming behind him. "All of you, please."

"Welcome home, Your Highness," Thoralf bowed deep, though the corner of his lips were having a hard time staying still. He glanced at Sybil and this time, he didn't stop the grin from spreading on his face. *Odin's beard, man, what have you gotten yourself into?* he added through their mental link.

Thoralf was his oldest friend and they grew up like brothers, having been a ward of the Royal Family since childhood, so he was used to his ribbing. *I wish I knew, my friend,* he answered back. *I wish I knew.*

"Welcome back, Your Highness," Rorik, second-in-command, greeted as he filed in behind Thoralf. At nearly seven feet tall, he was the tallest of the guard, though he wasn't as wide and intimidating as Stein, but Aleksei supposed it was difficult to look fearsome when one had wild red hair and twinkling green eyes. *Aleksei, I am happy for you. Envious, but thoroughly happy that you have found the other half of your soul.*

Thank you, Rorik. Aleksei nodded to the two men behind him.

They were identical in looks, with their white-blond hair and dark amber eyes, but the twin dragons were as different as night and day.

"I hope you had a pleasant journey, Your Highness." Gideon bowed deep, his eyes lowering to the floor in respect.

"He sure did," Niklas chuckled, his gaze immediately going to Sybil. "Well now, you've really done well for yourself, you lucky bas—"

"Niklas," Thoralf scolded. "You do not speak to His Highness that way when there are others present." *At least not out loud, you idiot,* he added.

"She's not just anyone," Niklas shot back. "She's his—"

Aleksei cleared his throat loudly. "*Gentlemen.* Shall we proceed?" *And let's stay out of each other's heads for the time being.*

Thoralf shot Niklas a warning look. "Of course. Stein is with His Majesty while he is meeting with the Minister of Agriculture."

"Good." At least one of the Dragon Guard always had to be with the king, as per security protocol. Usually it was at least three and most of the time it was all of them, but within the palace walls, King Harald was safe. "At ease."

That was his signal that they could do without the formalities. Niklas and Rorik visibly relaxed, and Gideon adapted a looser stance. Thoralf stepped forward. "So, Aleksei, you have a lot to catch us up on."

Aleksei stood and walked over to Sybil. Her dark brows were drawn together in curiosity. "As I've told Thoralf, this is

Sybil Lennox and she'll be our guest for the time being." He was careful not to use the word mate, but hopefully Thoralf had already told them. He quickly introduced each of the Dragon Guard by name.

"Nice to meet you all," she said.

Niklas whistled. "I've never met a female dragon before."

"Don't talk like she's not here, you dumbass," Gideon retorted. "Excuse my language, Miss Lennox. Bad habit I picked up at CalTech. Er," he stammered. "Not that I think Americans curse too much."

"Anyway," Aleksei continued. "Miss Lennox's life is in danger. The Knights mean to use The Wand on her." Though he had already spoken with Thoralf on the way here, he quickly brought the others up-to-date about what happened with The Knights. "She will be staying here for the time being."

"There's no other place safer, my lady," Thoralf said. "We shall protect you."

"We've agreed that she should keep her identity a secret for now," Aleksei said. "We will not mention that she's a Lennox. Or a dragon."

"That should keep some of the attention off of her," Gideon said. "But, unless you plan to keep her confined to her quarters, people will start talking."

"Gideon is right," Rorik said, his bushy red eyebrows moving up and down as he looked at Sybil. "We should come up with a story of why she is here, something believable."

Sybil thought for a moment. "Aleksei, how about we tell them I'm … the sister of your roommate from Oxford? And I'm visiting?"

"Excellent idea." His mate was gorgeous *and* smart, and his inner dragon preened, as if to tell him, *of course she is.*

"We shall certainly keep her identity a secret," Thoralf said.

"And that will be your main task." Sybil didn't need guarding from The Knights, after all. Not here. He already felt a hundred times better, knowing she was safe between the palace walls. "But, you must keep prying eyes away from her and squash any rumors. And for now, you must make sure she does not interact with any other shifters, in case they figure out what she is."

"Hopefully she can control her dragon," Niklas added.

"Can you guys please not talk as if I'm not here?" Sybil said in an annoyed voice. "And I can control my dragon fine, thank you very much."

"It's not you we are worried about, my lady," Thoralf said. "Once you are near other male dragons, they will certainly be, uh, curious."

Aleksei squashed the jealousy that was rearing its ugly head. His dragon did *not* like the idea of other male dragons near Sybil. His friends, he trusted with his life, but the others around them … he just hoped they wouldn't have to encounter any other dragons or shifters.

"We'll be beating them off with sticks, if they even get a whiff of you or get a hint of your lovely … charms," Niklas remarked with a grin.

"Just how many dragons are there around here?" Sybil asked.

"A small part of our population are dragons," Rorik said. "Though, we used to be numerous. And some other types of shifters, like wolves and deer. They live all over the Isles, though they do come to the castle often."

"Are we expecting any of the dragon families soon?" Aleksei asked.

"None of the dragon families," Thoralf said. *But there might be some ... other complications,* he added.

Complications? Aleksei frowned at him.

Jarl Solveigson will be dining with the King tonight.

"Complications." Niklas snorted. "*Right.*"

"Excuse me?" Sybil said.

Aleksei sent them all a warning mental message. "Uh, nothing to worry about." He walked over to his desk and picked up the phone, then dialed an extension. "Yes, it's me. She's ready, if you don't mind coming to my office. Excellent. Thank *you*." He put the phone down. "Sybil, Ursula will be by to fetch you in a minute. She'll take you to your room and attend to your needs."

"Are you throwing me out of your little meeting?" She raised a brow at him and crossed her arms under her breasts.

"No, we're done," he lied. "I just want to make sure you're refreshed and ready when you meet my father. He wishes to have a private audience with you before dinner in his study."

"Oh." Sybil's demeanor changed. Her gaze shifted from side to side.

"Do not worry." He came closer to her and longed to hold her to reassure her. He settled on placing his hands on her shoulders. "You will be fine."

"Thanks," she said.

"Your Highness?" A woman appeared at the doorway. When Aleksei turned to her, she made a deep curtsy. "Welcome back."

"Ursula." He took Sybil by the hand and brought her over. "This is Miss Sybil ... Brighton. Miss Brighton, this is Ursula Andresson."

Ursula's gaze immediately went to Sybil and Aleksei's linked hands and then to him. Her blue eyes danced with amusement as she looked at Aleksei meaningfully. "Lovely to meet you, Miss Brighton."

"Same here, Ms. Andresson."

"Let me show you to your rooms." Ursula gently pulled her away from Aleksei. It was a good thing the older woman was like a mother to Aleksei, otherwise, his dragon would have been furious at being separated from their mate.

"I shall come and fetch you in two hours," Aleksei said as they left. As soon as the door closed behind them, he turned back to the room.

"If you don't mind my saying," Thoralf began as he approached Aleksei. "Your mate is lovely as a spring day in the Dieldra Mountains. You are one lucky man."

"And she seems feisty too," Niklas added.

"When I asked him what your mate was like, Stein said she was 'spirited'." Gideon scratched his head. "I think he was impressed."

Rorik roared in laughter. "I imagine Stein would be impressed with any woman who didn't run in the opposite direction when they first lay eyes on him."

"I don't envy your position tonight, though." Thoralf patted him on the shoulder.

Aleksei had almost forgotten and he rubbed a palm down his face. "There are three hundred and sixty-five nights a year, and tonight had to be the night Jarl Solveignson is coming to dinner."

"Do you think there's a chance Lady Vera will be staying home?" Thoralf said hopefully.

Aleksei snorted. "Only if hell should freeze over."

CHAPTER TWELVE

SYBIL FOLLOWED URSULA, her heels click-clacking on the tiles as they walked down the long hallways. The older woman was dressed in a dark-colored pantsuit and her white-blonde hair was bound up in a neat bun. Still, despite her formal appearance, she was stunning and her face was youthful; Sybil guessed she must be in her late thirties, but from the way Aleksei talked about her, it sounded like she was the same age as his mother, which meant she had to have been at least ten years older.

"I hope your trip was all right? You aren't too tired, are you?" Ursula asked in the clipped accented voice Sybil had observed from the few people she met. Aleksei too, had the same lilting tone but not as obvious; his accent was much more posh, and she realized that was probably from his Oxford education.

"It was long," she said. "But the trip was all right."

"We'll have you refreshed in no time," she said. "Aleksei mentioned that perhaps you might not have any proper attire for dinner?"

"Yes, I'm afraid this was kind of a last-minute trip." Well, that was kind of true.

If Ursula was curious about the nature of Sybil's trip, she didn't show it. "Don't worry." She patted a hand on her arm. "I'll find you something stunning."

"Oh, I hope it's not a bother. Just something simple will do."

"Oh hush," Ursula chuckled. "It's not every day His Highness brings someone special for a visit."

"I'm not—"

"I've never seen him look at anyone the way he looks at you," she tutted. "And I don't believe his story about you being *just* the sister of a dear friend. But, I'm not wanting to gossip, and I know navigating such things can be ... delicate."

Sybil swallowed hard. There was no hiding anything from this woman, but how much did she suspect? Was she one of the traditionalists Aleksei had been talking about? Would she still be nice if she knew who Sybil really was?

As Ursula led her down a maze of hallways and steps, she explained some of the history of the castle, from the time it was built by the very first King of the Northern Isles, Hagard I, around 790 A.D. She listened with rapt attention, fascinated at how old everything was, especially compared to the United States.

"I hope I haven't bored you too much," Ursula said.

"Oh, not at all. It's all extremely interesting."

They stopped at one of the doors. "This is your room." Ursula opened the door and led her inside. "I hope it's comfortable."

Sybil looked around, her eyes growing wide. This room was probably four times the size of her entire apartment in

Blackstone and decorated ornately in blues and gold. "It's amazing. Probably too much."

Ursula gave her a sly smile. "We don't use this guest room much, since it is the closest to Prince Aleksei's private bedroom. His Highness' room is at the end of the hall and we have no other guests at the moment." She cleared her throat. "And since His Highness moved to the Crown Prince's apartments, no one else has used this guest room, or any of the adjoining ones."

"Oh." Heat crept up her neck at the implication.

"I'll have a few dresses sent up to you, Miss Brighton. If you need anything please do give me a call." She gestured to the phone on the bedside table. "The operator has been instructed to direct your call either to me or His Highness."

"Thank you, Ms. Andresson."

"It's absolutely my pleasure, Miss Brighton." Ursula bowed her head and gracefully headed toward the door.

As soon as she was alone, Sybil let out the breath she had been holding. Everything had been so different and foreign, and while she was around Aleksei it wasn't that bad, now that she was alone, it was closing in on her.

It's all right, she told herself. *It's going to be all right.*

Maybe she should have stayed home. She didn't realize how coming here would complicate things—and her feelings for Aleksei. She knew he was a prince, but there was so much more she was discovering about him. And now that she was in his territory and he was in his element, he seemed much more larger-than-life.

Her emotions were like a freight train she couldn't stop. And yet, she wasn't sure she wanted them to.

A knock on the door interrupted her thoughts. "Come in,"

she called. The door opened and two women came in, dragging two racks filled with dresses in all colors and fabrics.

"Miss Brighton," one of them said, "My name is Ulla. I'll be assisting you in getting ready."

"Hello, Ulla, nice to meet you," she said, then turned to the other woman. "And you are?"

The young woman blushed, then covered her mouth with her hand, her eyes darting over to Ulla.

"You must excuse Brigitta," Ulla said. "She is not confident in her English speaking skills yet, but she can understand it."

"Oh, I'm sorry," she said. "What language do you speak here? Is it Norwegian? Swedish?"

"Our native language is called Nordgensprak," Ulla said. "But really, it is a mix of Swedish and Finnish, with a bit of Icelandic. However, King Harald adopted English as an official language about ten years ago and so our school system has been trying to teach it and we have been integrating it into our day to day lives."

"Interesting." No wonder Aleksei had been sent to school in England; his father probably saw the usefulness of the language.

"If I may, Miss Brighton," Ulla gestured to the racks, "I've brought a few outfits for you to try, but would you allow me to suggest you some?"

Sybil's eyes glossed over all the dresses. Growing up, she'd never really been a fashionista type and she was glad for the help. "Yes, please."

"We don't have much time." Ulla spoke a few words to Brigitta, and the other woman nodded and then took out a train case. "But we will do our best."

Sybil hoped that whatever the Royal Family was paying Ulla and Brigitta, it was enough. They were miracle workers; or rather, fairy godmothers, as she felt like Cinderella. They tried on a few dresses, but finally settled on an outfit. At first glance, the blue-green dress seemed plain, with a scoop neckline and sleeves that came down to her elbows. But, it was backless and showed off the smooth skin and the delicate line of her spine. The mermaid skirt hugged her hips and showed off her ass. Brigitta styled her hair to one side and held it with jeweled clips to show off her back, and applied just a touch of makeup, saying a few soft words in a lilting tone.

"Brigitta says that you don't need a lot of makeup," Ulla translated. "You have beautiful skin and features."

"Thank you ... I mean, *tack*," Sybil answered, remembering the word for thank you.

The two women excused themselves as soon as they finished, and had left about fifteen minutes ago. It was nearly time for her to meet King Harald, and she was a bundle of nerves. What would he be like? She imagined someone cold or formal. Aleksei had only mentioned his father casually, but nothing about what he was like. She wished that they had spoken more; even if King Harald hated the thought that she was a Lennox, she could have at least prepared herself.

A soft knock interrupted her thoughts and she recognized Aleksei's voice call her name. The butterflies in her stomach fluttered and she wrapped an arm around her middle, trying to calm down. With a deep breath, she opened the door.

"Hi." She kept her eyes cast downward, looking up slowly until she looked up at his face. Aleksei looked especially handsome in his black tux, and with his long hair brushed and tied back. His jaw was freshly shaven and she got a whiff of cologne mixed in with his natural scent. Her mouth felt dry and her knees wobbled at the sight of him. Her dragon too, was pleased.

Mine. Mate.

"You look beautiful." The timbre of his voice sent her nerves tingling and she could feel the heat of his gaze. His hand reached for her, then, much to her surprise, he drew it back. "We should go, my father is waiting," he said in a clipped tone.

"Oh, right." Aleksei was acting weird. Maybe he was as nervous as she was? That was it.

He stepped aside to let her pass, and when she turned her back to him, she heard him let out a breath and mutter something unintelligible. Even without looking at him, she knew he saw her bare back and she felt some satisfaction at the reaction she had elicited from him.

She took two steps forward, then turned her head and smiled. "Are you coming?"

His shoulders straightened. "Yes. Of course."

They walked side by side, though Aleksei didn't make a move to guide her with a hand on her lower back, as he usually did. In fact, he stayed about a foot away from her and he didn't say a word; instead, his face was drawn into a scowl.

Sybil was pretty sure she had showered beforehand, so that wouldn't be why he was keeping his distance. *Hmm.* Now that she thought about it, she couldn't even remember the last time he had touched her. Maybe when they held hands as they passed through the magical veil. At one point during the flight, he had leaned over and she thought he was going to kiss her. And before that, there was that kiss. That soul-searing, aching kiss that made her toes curl just thinking about it. He said he wanted her, and that it didn't matter if she was a virgin. Then he brought her here and put her up in the room next to his, but now he was acting like she had some kind of disease.

And they said women sent mixed signals.

"We are here," Aleksei announced as they stopped in front of an ornate wooden door. Two men—whom she recognized as Stein and either Gideon or Niklas—stood on either side of the door. Neither moved nor acknowledged them as Aleksei opened the door and stepped in.

There was a small drawing room on the other side, and there was a man standing there. For a second, she was confused as this man was too young to be Aleksei's father.

"Hello, Erik," Aleksei said. "May I introduce you to my cousin, Prince Erik. Erik, this is Sybil."

"Nice to meet you, Sybil."

Sybil could see the similarities between the cousins, though Erik had dark hair and brown eyes as opposed to Aleksei's more fair features. Obviously, Erik was a dragon as well, though his animal wasn't as dominant as Aleksei's or even any of the Dragon Guard. He was handsome in that conventional way, she supposed, though his easy smile put her at ease.

"Lovely to meet you as well, Your Highness."

"Erik is aware of the situation," Aleksei said. "We'd spoken before I came to fetch you."

"Your secret is safe with me, Miss 'Brighton,'" he said.

"Father is eager to meet you." Aleksei nodded to the door on the other side of the waiting room. "We should go before he storms out here and demands to have a look at you."

Sybil followed Aleksei and Erik inside. Like the rest of the palace, this room was just as richly decorated and ornate. Her gaze immediately went to the tall figure standing by the window, his back facing them.

"Father," Aleksei called as they neared. "May I present, Miss Sybil Lennox."

He turned around and Sybil felt her heart stop for a second. She could see where Aleksei got his looks from—he was the spitting image of his father. King Harald was the same height and broad like his son, with the same light brown hair, albeit cut short and had streaks of gray at the temple.

"My dear Miss Lennox." The wrinkles at the corner of his eyes deepened as his face broke into a grin. "I've been eager to meet you."

Sybil curtsied. "Your Majesty." She'd practiced a few times with Ulla and Brigitta and they assured her that she was doing it correctly. "Thank you for your hospitality."

"The situation that has brought you so suddenly is a terrible one." He took her hand and brought her up. "But I assure you, you are most welcome here."

As she looked up at his blue-green eyes, she couldn't help but feel the power of his dragon. It wasn't quite the same as Aleksei's, but just as strong, maybe even more. Perhaps because he wasn't just alpha, but also King. "Thank you just the same."

His eyes searched hers, as if assessing her. "My, my ... extraordinary." He looked at Aleksei. "Is she really your—"

"Yes, Father." He cleared his throat. "But perhaps we can talk about other things."

"For now." His eyes sparkled. "I hope you're comfortable with your accommodations? And that you have everything you need?"

"Yes, Your Majesty. Everyone I've met has been kind and extremely helpful, especially Ursula, Ulla, and Brigitta." She hoped that helped the last two women score some points with the king.

"I'm glad we have a few minutes alone before dinner," King Harald said. "My son has informed me of the background story you have come up with. I assure you that you will be safe from our enemies here, I guarantee it personally, but perhaps to prevent tongues from wagging, it would be best we keep with that story, for now at least." He lowered his voice. "Of course, you are free to do as you please, in *private—*"

"*Father.*" Aleksei's tone was warning, but not impertinent.

"What?" King Harald said, then wiggled his eyebrows at his son in a very *un-royal* way. This made Aleksei sigh deeply and roll his eyes. Sybil suspected they were doing that mental link thing. Curiosity pricked at her, wondering what they were saying to each other. Erik, on the other hand, flashed her a meaningful smile.

"Let's not keep our guests waiting, Father," Aleksei said.

"All right," he sighed deeply. "Perhaps tomorrow I shall arrange a private tour of the estates for you, my dear." He turned to his son. "Let's get on with it, shall we?"

King Harald walked ahead of them, and as he passed by the two guards, Stein followed behind. As Sybil tried to walk ahead of Aleksei, she felt a hand on her arm.

"Excuse me, Miss Brighton." Based on the soft, polite tone, Sybil guessed this was Gideon. "Protocol dictates that Prince Erik, then Prince Aleksei shall enter the dining room first, followed by His Majesty, The King."

"Gideon will show you to the dining room," Aleksei said. "Do not worry, I had Ursula place you next to me."

Gideon's eyebrow shot up, which Aleksei answered with a glare. The other man looked like he wanted to protest, but bowed.

Sybil knew they were definitely doing the mind link thing.

"Anything to share with the class, gentlemen?" she said in a sarcastic tone.

"Apologies," Aleksei said. "But, if you don't mind, we really must go."

"Fine. Let's go."

CHAPTER THIRTEEN

"Is the food not to your liking, Miss Brighton?" Jarl Einer Solveigson asked.

Sybil looked up to her right as she pushed her potatoes around her plate. "It's fine, My Lord. I'm just tired from the long trip."

"Perhaps she is one of those Americans who don't eat carbs," a cutting voice said from across the table. "How wasteful."

Sybil's head whipped toward the speaker. Lady Vera Solveigson smiled back at her, but it didn't quite reach her eyes. In fact, from the way she bared her teeth, she looked downright feral. For a moment, Sybil wondered if she really was human.

Jarl Solveigson let out a forced laugh. "Oh, my dear daughter, such a comedian." He seemed almost nervous as his gaze darted toward Aleksei. "I'm sure Miss Brighton is just not used to such new things."

"As a *foreigner*, I'm sure she's not used to many things around here," Vera added.

Sybil wondered what the punishment was for wringing someone's neck during dinner in the Northern Isles. It probably wasn't kosher, but she'd been wanting to do it all night, ever since she met Lady Vera.

When Gideon brought her to the dining room, Ursula had a footman escort her to her chair, which was right beside Aleksei's, but to her surprise, it was already occupied. The pretty young woman sitting on the chair smiled up at her innocently and pointed to the place card in front of her that said "Lady Vera Solveigson." Meanwhile, the card with Sybil's name was across the table, one chair down.

The footman looked appalled and apologized, and asked her to wait for a moment, muttering under his breath. Sybil didn't realize this at the time, but there was some sort of protocol involved with the seating, plus the poor young man obviously didn't want to cause a scene. The head butler came out a minute later, looking cool as a cucumber, but his tightly fisted hands showed his frustration.

"It appears that one of my staff has made a mistake with the placement of the name cards, Lady Vera," the butler had said. "My deepest apologies."

"Oh?" Vera batted her eyes and placed a hand over her heart. "You really must train them better then. Perhaps you should have the man sacked."

"I shall certainly speak with them, but Lady Vera—"

"Yes?" Vera had leaned back in her chair and made herself comfortable.

"You must ... I mean ..."

Sybil had sensed the butler's frustration. This really wasn't worth all the fuss. "It's all right, Mr.—"

"Birgir, ma'am. Just Birgir." Though his face remained impassive, she could sense his distress.

"Birgir, then." She smiled at him, trying to put him at ease. "I'm sure my seat is fine." She gave a fake shiver. "It's quite cold in here and I'm looking forward to being warm by the fire." She nodded at her place, which was nearer to the fireplace. "Thank your staff for being so sensitive to my needs." And with that, she had taken her seat.

Sybil had a bad feeling about the whole thing, but she didn't know how correct her instincts were. Now, it was plain as day: Lady Vera had switched her place cards so that *she* could be seated next to Aleksei, not Sybil. And to make matters worse, she had to watch from across the table as Vera flirted shamelessly with Aleksei during the dinner, laughing at his jokes, hanging on to every word, and even giving him touches here and there.

Mine. Mate. Her dragon seethed, and the fire was building inside her again. Maybe she wouldn't wring Vera's neck, but instead toss a fireball at her perfectly styled long blonde hair.

Not that Aleksei minded, a voice inside her said. Aleksei didn't say anything when he walked in and saw he was sitting down next to Vera. Instead, he was perfectly calm, standing and waiting as his father's arrival was announced, before sitting down for the dinner service. He even alternated speaking with her, his father, Erik—who sat on King Harald's left—and Jarl Solveigson, who was seated beside Erik. There were also a few other people dining with them, mostly minor ministers and their wives. According to Ursula, it was not a state dinner, which is why they were in the more private King's Dining Room; but rather, a formal meal that the king sometimes had to keep the nobles and politicians happy.

Erik turned to face her. "I'm sure Miss Brighton will soon enjoy everything the Northern Isles has to offer." He gave her a saucy wink, one that no one else saw.

"We don't get many *outsiders* here." Vera narrowed her eyes. "Why are you visiting here again, Miss Brighton?"

"She was traveling with her brother, Liam. Then they were supposed to come here together." Finally, Aleksei acknowledged she existed, albeit indirectly. "But he was delayed on business and my friend urged that she continue on with their planned trip to visit. I was happy enough to accommodate one of my dearest and oldest friends."

Sybil took a sip of her wine and swallowed the bitter liquid. "Right. Just doing a friend a favor."

King Harald cleared his throat. "That was an excellent dinner, was it not?" He stood up, which sent everyone scrambling up from their seats. "I invite you all to coffee, digestifs, and other refreshments in the drawing room. Unfortunately, I have an early day tomorrow and I will be retiring. But please, don't let my absence stop you from enjoying what we have to offer." He said a few more words in Nordgensprak, then strode out of the dining room, Stein and Gideon following right behind him.

"Your Highness," Vera said in a breathless voice. "Do you suppose the Royal Kitchens prepared that divine vanilla custard I had the last time I was here?"

"I'm afraid I didn't see the menu for the evening, Lady Vera."

She looked up sweetly at him. "Then let's find out, shall we?"

Sybil had to rein in her dragon tightly when she saw Vera's claw-like hands dig into Aleksei's bicep. She felt heat rise up her cheeks and all the way to the tips of her ears. Unable to take any more, she pivoted on her heel.

"Sybil?"

She stopped and turned. "Prince Erik?"

"Are you not joining us in the drawing room?"

"I feel a headache coming on," she said glumly. "Would it be rude or break protocol if I left now?"

"No, of course not," he said. "If the King himself retires, then the guests are free to do so as well."

She breathed a sigh of relief. "Thank you."

"Of course. Shall I send Ursula or the royal physician up to you?"

"No need," she said. "I have some pain killers in my bag. I probably just need some sleep too."

He nodded. "Have a good evening."

"You too." Sybil turned, wanting to leave the dining room immediately. No, she wanted to leave this *palace* entirely. Jealousy reared its ugly head, but she couldn't lash out. Maybe she could just fly away. For now, she satisfied the urge to run by stomping out of the dining room.

What had changed exactly? It was like the minute they landed here, Aleksei had turned into a completely different person. He treated her like she was some stranger. During dinner, he wouldn't even acknowledge her. And, as much as she hated to admit it, it had *hurt*.

"Damn!" She stopped suddenly. In her haste, she had started walking down one of the hallways and was now lost. "Double damn." She wrinkled her brow, trying to remember the landmarks. There was that painting of some grand lady in a white dress that was at the end of the hallway before her bedroom. Or was it the man with the mustache?

"Sybil."

She froze at the sound of the familiar voice from behind her. "You found me."

"*Lyubimaya*, I will always find you."

His footsteps drew nearer but she didn't turn around.

"What are you doing following me anyway?" she huffed. "Wasn't the Lady Vera's company enough for you?"

He dared to chuckle. "Are you jealous, Sybil?"

"Jealous?" Her voice rose a few decibels louder than she wanted. "I. Am. Not. Jealous." She turned around to face him, just to show him how decidedly *not* jealous she was.

His eyes shifted from amusement to tenderness. "There is nothing to be jealous about." He drew her into his arms and she didn't have the strength to resist. Or didn't want to. She melted against him, her hands moving up to his shoulders as he bent down to kiss her.

The touch of his lips was just as electrifying as the first time they kissed. His mouth moved over hers in a sensuous caress, as he pressed his body close to hers. Oh God, she wanted him so bad she could scream. The lust she felt was real and it was driving her crazy.

Her hands found the front of his jacket and she unbuttoned it impatiently. She felt him smile against her mouth and maneuver her backwards until she was trapped against the wall. He pressed his body against hers, letting her feel the evidence of his desire through their clothes. Moving his mouth from hers, he rained kisses down her cheek, to her jawline, and to the exposed section of her neck, suckling at the delicate bare skin.

She gasped when she felt the dampness between her legs, and she spread her knees to get him closer. Thrills of excitement ran through her, and the touch of fear only made her want him more. "Aleksei, please. Can we be alone? In your room. Or mine. I don't care." She was so ready for this.

He stopped that delicious thing he was doing with his mouth. "Sybil, I'm sorry. I cannot."

It was like she jumped into a cold lake. *No. Not again.* She wrenched herself from him. "Then stop making me feel this way, then tossing me aside like some piece of garbage!" she hissed.

"No! Sybil." He grasped her before she could get away and then trapped her in his arms. "No, listen, please. Don't *say* that." He pressed his lips to her temple.

As warmth began to pool in her belly, her eyelids dropped, but she snapped them open. "Is it Vera?"

"What about her?" When she remained silent, he continued. "She is from one of our richest and noblest families. Her father spoils her rotten and gives her anything she wants." He sighed. "For some reason, she has set her eyes on me and Jarl Solveigson has been trying to cater to this particular whim by trying to win me, and my father's favor, but ... there is nothing between us, I assure you."

"It's not just that," she said, unable to meet his gaze. "Since we came here, you've been different. It's like ... it's like I'm nobody to you."

"Do not say that, Sybil. You are not nobody. I'm sorry I made you feel that way." He loosened his grip, but didn't let go. "Don't you think I want to shout to everyone in that room, in the entire country, that you're mine? That I found the one person who truly is the other half of my soul? But I can't. Not yet."

"I'm safe here, you said. So, I know you're not trying to protect me from The Knights." She chewed on her lip. "Is it because I'm a Lennox?" Maybe he suddenly realized that he couldn't be with her in any way. The history between their families ran too deep. "Have you changed your mind since we came here?"

"Never," he whispered.

"Then why don't you want me?"

"Not want you?" He laughed. "How can you think that? Haven't I been telling you all this time how much I want you? You are *lyubimaya moya*." He leaned down, whispering into her ear. "My beloved."

Her heart banged against her rib cage and her throat went dry. Was he saying—

"That day The Knights attacked you, I was trying to tell you something. When I said to you that you would be more than a romp in the sheets. I wanted you to be absolutely sure about being with me. I want you to be mine, to accept the mating bond and truly be my mate. My wife and my princess, and future Queen."

Oh my God. Was he proposing? Fear and anxiety suddenly shot through her.

"See? Even now, you hesitate. I can see it in your eyes. You're not sure yet that you want me."

"But I do want you," she said quickly, despite her mind protesting at the thought of being trapped. She wrapped her arms around his neck to bring him closer.

"Sybil," he gently unwound her arms, "it would be dishonorable for me to simply take my pleasure from your body without anything between us."

Hold on. When the realization hit her, she wanted to laugh. "You want to wait until marriage?"

"Your body, innocent that it may be, wants me," he said. "But I will not have you until you give your all to me. Body. Heart. Soul."

His words were like a vice, gripping her body and making her feel claustrophobic. She knew what he wanted. He wanted her to say she would be his mate and stay here. And it became clear why she hesitated.

She had wanted for a mate for so long, it never occurred to

her that he wouldn't be from back home. Being with Aleksei would mean never living in Blackstone again, and leaving her job, her life, her family. Her days and nights would be endless formal dinners and balls, and smiling for his people. Never having privacy, never being just herself.

And that thought terrified her.

"Aleksei, can't we just … take it slow? We need to get to know each other first. It's barely been a week." She moved closer to try and tempt him.

"Slow?" he asked. "Does this pace not feel glacial to you? Does your dragon not long to be with its mate? To bond with us and be with us for the rest of our lives?"

Her dragon answered in the affirmative, of course.

Mine. Mate.

And his answered back, a roar that deafened her ears and shook her to her very core. Still, she said her next words carefully. "I don't … I don't even know how this mate bonding works. Everyone just says it'll happen."

"According to our history," he began, "when two fated mates have accepted each other and love flows between them, then the mating bond occurs. It binds them, makes them stronger, and makes them one."

It was obvious what he was asking. What he was telling her in so many words. But, did she feel that way for him already?

He looked defeated when she didn't answer. "Come, *lyubimaya*." He offered his arm and she took it. "I will take you to your room and I will retire as well."

"Your guests—"

"Erik is taking care of them. We will rest and then tomorrow, my father has arranged a small outing for us. He wants to show you something special. Something few people, even those from here, have seen."

"He does? What is it?"

"It's a surprise. Now," he guided her down the hallway. "These hallways are tricky, and I swear, when I was younger and I got lost, I thought they moved on their own."

As they made their way back to his apartments, he began to tell her some stories from his childhood. She listened to him, but his earlier words replayed in the back of her mind. She wanted him so bad, and she couldn't believe he was turning her down because it was dishonorable. *If Kate were here, she'd be saying something about me having a case of blue balls.*

Finally, after a long, agonizing walk back, where it was like all she could think about was how good he smelled or how hard his bicep was under her fingers, they reached her room.

"Good night, *lyubimaya*," he said, leaning down to press his lips to her cheek. "I wish you good dreams."

Her shoulders sank as he walked away, and she had no choice but to go into her room, listening to the sound of his footsteps getting fainter and fainter.

This is my life, she thought glumly. She'd been waiting for the one man who wouldn't be afraid of her name or her animal to come and take away her pesky virginity, and he ... wanted to wait until marriage. She thumped her head softly against the door. She really had the worst luck when it came to men.

She straightened her spine and turned to the room. There wasn't really much she could do at this point, was there? Aleksei was firm on his stance: no mating, no sex. Was she just supposed to declare her love for him, when she had all these doubts in her mind? Couldn't they first figure out if they were compatible? And for God's sake, if she didn't get *anything* from him, she was afraid her body would just burst.

Feeling defeated, she grabbed her suitcase. She hadn't even unpacked. Her comfy pajamas and a good night's sleep would do her good.

As she opened the suitcase, Sybil noticed a package wrapped in a plain white tissue sitting on top of her folded clothes. "Huh." She picked it up and saw the familiar, feminine scrawl that said *"Negotiate."*

Curious, she unraveled the package and gasped as her fingers grasped something silky and soft. *Hmmm.* Negotiate indeed.

Sybil's heart was hammering in her chest as she stood outside Aleksei's door. It was obvious *what* the package Riva had snuck into her suitcase was for, but she wondered if her mother had ever thought it would be so she could seduce Aleksei because he was the one holding out before they were married.

The negligee was almost old-fashioned, with a long, red silky skirt that fell down to her toes. But the entire top was made of red lace, covering only the necessary bits and leaving tantalizing glimpses of skin bare. A silk ribbon around her neck held everything in place and one tug would take it all off.

She nearly chickened out, but she put it on and told herself that she had to use every bit of advantage she had if she was going to get Aleksei to sleep with her. Because she damn well wasn't waiting until marriage. What if they weren't compatible? Or what if she realized she didn't want to be queen? Or what if she didn't like sex with Aleksei?

Her dragon snorted at the silly notion.

Oh, shut up.

As she waited by the door, she didn't know if she should knock, but then again, that would kind of ruin the surprise, right? So, she scrunched up every bit of courage she could and pushed it open.

"Aleksei?" she whispered. "Are you here?"

Her shifter eyes adjusted to the darkness in the room and her gaze was immediately drawn to the large bed in the middle of the room. The sheets had been disturbed and pushed aside, but the bed was empty. Where was he?

A gust of wind made her turn and she saw the sheer curtain flapping in the breeze, as if calling her. *Ah, he probably went out to his balcony.* With careful steps, she walked over to the door. When she pushed the curtain aside, she gasped.

It wasn't a balcony. Well, it was a balcony, but it was also apparently a swimming pool. An enormous pool at that. It was similar to the balcony off her parent's room in the castle, as it had to be big enough to accommodate her father's dragon when he needed to take off. The half-moon in the sky reflected across the surface, then distorted as a wave rippled by. Her breath caught in her throat when she saw a fin surface from the water. Aleksei. Of course, this pool could fit him in his dragon form.

She saw part of a scaled body rise up from the water and then disappear. A few seconds later, a head appeared right by her feet. Startled, she jumped back.

"Sybil?" Aleksei looked confused, but when his gaze dropped down to what she was wearing, his eyes turned dark. His palms slapped on the edge and he hauled himself up, sending water spilling over. He moved as graceful as a cat, stalking toward her.

When she realized that he was fully naked, she couldn't help but devour the sight of his body with her eyes. His skin was slick with water and rivulets poured down, dragging her gaze along as the droplets dripped over his well-formed pecs, his washboard abs, and lower still, to his fully erect cock. For a moment, she felt real fear, but also excitement. She'd seen naked men before, but not quite like this. Not, quite literally, *in the flesh.*

"What are you doing here?" he asked, his voice rough with desire.

"I came here to talk." She managed to drag her eyes up to his.

"You have made your decision?"

"I have made a ... realization." *Don't chicken out now, Sybil.*

He crossed his arms over his chest. "A realization?"

"Uh-huh." She stood her ground. "You've only stated what *you* want, but you never asked me what I want."

"Oh, so this is a negotiation?" He sounded amused. "All right, but first, you must join me."

"Join you where?"

He gestured to the pool. "In there. We can *negotiate* there."

"In your pool? That's your territory," she said. "That hardly seems fair."

"You come into my room, asking to talk, yet you wear *that.*" His gaze sent flames of desire licking up and down her body. "And you talk about fairness?"

"Well, you're naked," she retorted.

"And you came in unannounced. How was I supposed to know you would barge in here?"

Okay, she so could hardly fault that logic. "Fine." But she wasn't going down without a fight. She turned around and gathered her hair to one side. "I don't want to get this wet. You should undo me."

The brush of his fingers at her nape had her knees wobbling, but she tried to keep her nervousness from showing. When he undid the ribbon, the negligee slid down her body and pooled at her feet. The cold night air made gooseflesh prickle over her skin and her nipples tightened. She found the last bit of courage she had and stepped out from the circle of silk at her feet, then turned around to face him.

Aleksei's gaze blazed with lust, and she could see the muscle tick in his jaw and his spine grew stiff. She didn't miss the way his cock twitched, and she counted that as a small victory.

"Ladies first." He gestured to the pool.

"Thank you." She approached the edge, dipping her toes in experimentally. To her surprise, the water was warm.

"It is heated," he said. "I don't need it, but some nights it is more pleasant when the water is warmed."

As gracefully as she could, she got into the water, bending to sit down and sliding right in. "Oh." This was amazing. The water felt good on her chilled skin and—

A splash behind her made her startle. Before she could say anything, a pair of hands grabbed her arms, then pulled her to a wet, hard and very male body.

"I have decided on something, *lyubimaya*," Aleksei whispered in her ear.

Sybil tried to ignore the way his cock was pressing up against her ass. "Y-yes?"

He moved so gracefully and so fast in the water, she didn't even realize that he'd twisted her around so she was trapped against the edge of the pool. She squeaked, but he covered her mouth before she could protest further. *Oh, damn his delicious mouth!*

"You're right, it wasn't fair of me to impose restrictions on you," he said, moving his lips lower, over her jaw, down to her neck, until he disappeared under the water.

"Oh, yes." *Finally.* "Aleksei, yes!" She gripped the edge of the pool, using it to steady herself. Aleksei's mouth covered one nipple, teasing and lashing at it with his tongue. His other hand moved lower, between her thighs, spreading them as his fingers teased at her core.

A finger prodded at her entrance, and, finding her slick enough, slipped inside. "Oh God!" She moaned aloud, hoping that no one heard her, but didn't really care either way. She clenched around him, her hips bucking up to meet his hand as he continued to tease her nipple with his mouth.

The pleasure was mounting up inside her, threatening to spill over, when she realized that Aleksei was *underwater*. Oh, dear. He wasn't drowning either. Which meant—

"Damn!" Her body shuddered as she felt her climax wash over her. It felt like the waves lapping at her, but only inside her body. And Aleksei, that sneaky bastard, released her nipple and moved down lower. And, he didn't even come up for air.

He could breathe underwater.

He moved lower, licking a path down her belly, and then hooked her legs over his shoulders. She closed her thighs around his head.

"Oh! Aleksei!" She gripped the edge harder as she felt his tongue on her. His mouth clamped over her clit, sending her into a spiraling orgasm as he sucked on her and his fingers continued to move inside her, filling her, but making her ache for his cock to be inside her.

When her body began to calm down, Aleksei's head finally popped up in front of her. "Did you enjoy that, *lyubimaya?*"

"Uh-huh." She reached for him. "Now, take me to bed."

"I will," he said. "But not, mine. I shall escort you back to your rooms."

"What?" Her hazy, pleasure-soaked brain sobered. "What about you? Aren't you … Don't you want—"

He moved his lower body up against hers, so his hard cock brushed against her belly. "Never ask me again if I desire you, because you know the answer."

"But you said that you weren't going to have sex with me until after we got married. Clearly, we've crossed that line."

"I said *I* would not take pleasure from *you*," he reminded her. "But, I never said I would not give it to *you*. So, Sybil, I will give you as much pleasure as you want. Just ask."

"But you won't let me touch you," she finished.

"Not until you agree to give what I ask."

Damned bastard. "I can't … you'd really …" How could he think she would even let him suffer like that?

His reply was quick and decisive. "Yes."

Clearly, she'd been outmaneuvered. But then again, he probably had more experience in negotiations than she did. "Fine," she pouted. The orgasms he gave her had been mind-blowing, but she could hold out if he could. "But you don't know what you're missing out on."

It was like his gaze could penetrate the water as he stared down at her body. "Oh, I do. Believe me, I do, *lyubimaya*. But it will all be worth it."

CHAPTER FOURTEEN

ALEKSEI STOOD outside Sybil's door, fist held up to knock, but he didn't move. He hesitated, worried about how she would react to him this morning. He wondered if she would pretend last night didn't happen. But, at the same time, eager to see her again this morning.

Last night's Sybil was like the fire of her dragon: hot and burning bright. Her boldness tempted him, as did her sweet little body. He controlled himself, though his dragon and his cock were in agreement and had other ideas. He soothed his ache with a cold shower after he had escorted her to her room. It had worked, for at least a little while, but still, he couldn't erase the memory of her and how she tasted.

I must control myself. There was no compromise of negotiations—he would have all of her and he would wait. Because she was worth it. He had fallen so deeply in love with her, there was no other alternative. Hopefully, she would accept him before all this waiting killed him.

Finally, he knocked on the door. Three decisive raps before he called her name softly.

"Wait a minute," he heard her voice call out. He could hear her scrambling about the room, then walk closer to the door.

"Good morning," she said as she opened the door.

"Good morning." Today, she looked lovelier than ever. She was wearing another long sweater dress, but this time it was the color of rust, plus a pair of dark trousers underneath. The top she wore had a deep V and showed off a hint of cleavage and his mind traveled back to last night, when he held her bountiful breasts in his hands and teased her hard nipples. She merely stood there and yet she tempted him. He wanted to push her back in her bedroom and have his way with her, and plunge into her willing, delectable body.

And she was willing, as she had shown him. Last night, jealousy had been a catalyst for her to move forward. He had no choice but to be polite to Lady Vera, despite his irritation that the annoying little gnat had somehow switched places with Sybil. Still, he was an honorable man and would never manipulate Sybil intentionally with jealousy. No, she would come to him, of her own accord, and not because she was some child whose toy was stolen by another.

"Are you ready?" he asked, clearing his throat.

"Yes, but I hope this is okay." She gestured to her outfit. "I wasn't sure what to wear on a formal tour with a king."

A cute blush bloomed on her cheeks as his eyes roamed over her again. "It's fine. You are fine." He wanted to rip the sweater off of her, but bit his tongue before he could make a comment. "We should go. Father is waiting."

Automatically, Sybil stepped forward and linked her arm around him. Interesting. She didn't seem like she was playing games today. She seemed pleasant, her usual self at least, but he wondered what she was thinking about. Was her mind also on last night? He sincerely hoped so.

They walked out of his wing and back down to the garage. The nondescript van was already waiting for them, and Thoralf stood by the door. This was the vehicle his father used when he didn't want to be spotted, and today called for that. After all, this was going to be an important morning for them all.

Thoralf greeted him a good morning in his mind as he grabbed the door to open it. King Harald was already seated inside.

"Good morning, my dear," he said cheerfully. "I hope you had a good sleep."

"Good morning, Your Majesty. And I did, thank you for asking," Sybil said, another blush coming on and her eyes seemed to avoid Aleksei's. She took the seat beside King Harald. "May I ask, Your Majesty, where we are going today?"

His eyes sparkled with glee. "Ah, today I will show you our greatest treasures. Niklas," he called to his Dragon Guard and driver for the day. "I want to get started. Let's go."

"At once, Your Majesty." Niklas started the car and soon they were off.

Sybil seemed content enough to stare out the window, watching the scenery go by.

Do not fret, my boy, King Harald said through their mind link. *We will seal the deal today.*

Aleksei hoped his father didn't hear the inward groan in his head. This morning, he had barely woken up when he'd knocked on his door politely. Obviously, his father was being a nosy old man, wondering if he had bonded with Sybil yet. After all, since meeting her, all he wanted to know was when he was getting his dragonling grandchildren. He seemed mighty disappointed to have found his son alone in his room. Aleksei had invited his father in for a chat and told him (minus last night's events in the pool) that Sybil still had her reservations. King Harald had given him a pat on the back and said, "I shall take care of this."

And now, here they were, on the way to the Quarry. He wasn't sure what his father meant to do, but Aleksei doubted Sybil would be impressed enough to accept the mating bond by what she was about to see.

Soon, they were deep into the Middlelands, right in the heart of the Northern Isles. The roads had become unpaved, and a few miles later, they passed foreboding gates and reinforced steel walls.

"We're here," King Harald declared as the vehicle stopped. "Let's go."

They alighted from the van and Aleksei helped Sybil out. The van had stopped right outside the mouth of the Quarry. Two men waited outside, dressed in traditional Northern Isle armor. They stood ramrod straight, though they executed an impressive bow to one knee as King Harald walked by.

Sybil turned her head, watching the two guards. "Who are they?" He couldn't blame her, despite the feeling of jealousy rearing inside him. They did look splendid in their armor, plus both men were nearly seven feet tall.

"The Royal Quarry Guards," Aleksei said, his arm tightening on her elbow.

"Are they like the Dragon Guard?"

"Something like that. Except they do not guard the Royal Family." He guided her carefully as they walked over the slick and uneven stones.

"Then what do they guard? Is it—" Her eyes grew wide and she went slack-jawed the moment they entered the next room. "This is ..."

"Splendid, is it not?" King Harald gestured behind him. "Welcome to the Royal Quarry."

"This is some quarry," Sybil said. "Those are ... gemstones!"

Indeed, the walls of the Quarry were covered in all kinds of precious stones. They were mostly emeralds and sapphires, though they also found rubies and, much to their surprise, pearls. And these weren't just ordinary jewels. The smallest ones were the size of Aleksei's fist. They covered the entire cavern, which was about the size of the ballroom in the palace with walls about twenty feet high. And this was just the main corridor. The Quarry itself extended for miles underground, and were so vast that they had only finished mapping out the entire place a decade ago.

"This is our main natural resource," King Harald explained.

Sybil chuckled then turned to Aleksei. "I remember that day when Matthias was trying to insult you and you said the same thing about 'natural resources'. This certainly isn't just sticks and rocks. Why ... with all these gems ... you could probably buy Fort Knox five times over."

"It would attract a lot of attention," King Harald said.

"Which is why we prefer to keep our wealth a secret," Aleksei added. "If anyone were to find out ..."

"I can see that." Sybil still looked agog. "But ... how do you manage to sell it?"

"Our ancestors relied on the black market," Aleksei explained. "But with technology and such, we are able to use the Internet to put up hundreds of websites to sell to jewelers all over the world. We've been able to turn our treasure hoard quickly into cash, gold, stocks, bonds—"

"And a few shell companies and Swiss bank accounts to hide it all," Harald finished.

"Has this always been here from the beginning?" she asked him.

"As far back as our history goes, the secret passing from King to Crown Prince."

"As you've heard, dragons hoard treasure," Aleksei began. "Water Dragons hoard gemstones."

"In this case, however, our ancestors had already found this hoard and thus we are content to simply use them to care for our kingdom and our people."

"Except for a few prized pieces," King Harald said with a wink. "We are still dragons, after all."

"The bigger ones and the really exceptional pieces we keep in the hoard treasury or have them fashioned for use by the Royal Family."

"Wait, bigger than this?" Sybil pointed to the ruby the size of an ostrich's egg.

"*Much* bigger, my dear," King Harald said with a laugh.

"This is …" She held her hand out to touch the ruby. "May I?"

"Of course."

She touched the gem, running her palm over the stone. "This is incredible."

"Not as incredible as the way your family mines the blackstone," King Harald said.

"No, but this is different." Sybil gave a girlish laugh. "This is amazing. Thank you for showing this to me, Your Majesty. I promise to keep it a secret."

King Harald's eyes twinkled again. "This is a secret reserved only for the rulers of the Northern Isles, and the Dragon Guards."

Aleksei had to give his father credit. He was a clever one. Sybil bowed her head, but flashed Aleksei a dirty look.

"We could do a tour, but it's pretty much the same all over," King Harald said. "Besides, I have another event planned for us."

"An event?" Sybil asked.

"Yes. I thought it would be nice to have a gathering. A ... barbecue? Is that what you Americans call it? Like a picnic."

Sybil laughed. "Yes, a barbecue. Though we usually have those when the weather is warmer."

It was King Harald's turn to laugh. "My dear, this is warm in the Northern Isles. Besides, I think you will enjoy this gathering." He gave his son a meaningful look, but didn't send any message through their mind link. "At least, much more than last night's dinner."

As they approached the Royal Gardens, Aleksei still didn't know what to expect. His father had already told him about bringing Sybil to the Quarry, but not what he planned afterwards. He just hoped he hadn't arranged some fancy tea or soirée with more of the noble families or ministers. Something told him that Sybil would hate it, but would be too polite to say anything.

"Welcome to the Royal Gardens," King Harald said. "It was built to be a public place where people could come and enjoy the fresh air, the splendid flora, and outdoors in general, but sometimes we do close it for special functions, like today."

The gate to the Gardens was open, but cordoned off with a blue-green velvet rope. Thoralf moved the rope as they approached.

"Ah, good, they are already here," King Harald beamed.

Aleksei's eyes scanned over his father's guests. The

delighted shrieks of children filled the air. They seemed to be everywhere—running around the paths, climbing up the trees, playing hide and seek behind the topiaries. Then, there was a group of elderly people sitting under a tent, drinking tea, chatting, and playing card games. "Who exactly did you invite, Father?"

"I thought it would be nice to have a party for the recipients of the Queen's Trust," King Harald said. "These are the people who most need our help."

"It's a charity foundation?" Sybil asked.

"Yes. We like to take care of everyone in the Northern Isles, but we still do have some especially vulnerable people. The children are from some of the more disadvantaged families on the Isles. We provide for their needs through the Children's Foundation, while our elderly guests come from the senior community center and the local hospital." King Harald flashed a knowing glance at Aleksei. "Your family has a similar foundation, right? The Lennox Foundation? And I've been told that you yourself work for the government as a social worker."

Aleksei definitely hadn't mentioned anything about what Sybil did for a living, but he wasn't surprised. His father probably had Gideon gather as much information as he could about her the moment he told him about her being his mate.

"Would you like to meet them, my dear?" King Harald offered his arm.

"Of course." Sybil took it and allowed the older man to lead her, with Aleksei following behind. They walked over to the tent where there was also food being set up—some Northern Isle delicacies, but also a few American dishes he recognized, like potato salad and hot dogs. King Harald was met by an official-looking woman, the director of the Queen's

Trust, Magda Allenstrom. Magda introduced them to the managers of the Children's Foundation, the senior center, and the hospital. Afterwards, they all spent a significant amount of time meeting the elderly guests. It was good timing because it allowed the caretakers and volunteers from the Children's Foundation to round up the rambunctious children. King Harald laughed at the antics of the young ones. He seemed amused that they were not impressed by his presence and obviously just wanted to keep playing and running around.

As they mingled and spoke with the people at the barbecue, someone—one of the volunteers—had to run off to help one kid who was stuck in a tree. She handed Sybil one of their youngest charges: a child a few months old whose parents had died in a terrible fire. The baby survived, and now she lived under the care of the Queen's Trust.

"You work with children, correct?" King Harald asked, peering down at the baby in Sybil's arms.

"Oh, yes." She cooed at the child, tickling its nose, making her laugh.

Aleksei couldn't help the intense feeling that was coursing through his veins as he watched Sybil cuddle the baby. Of course, he was thinking of how beautiful she would look, with her stomach round with their child and eventually, holding his heir just like this. His dragon agreed wholeheartedly, and then gave a snort, probably one of disapproval at his idiotic stipulations.

We cannot dishonor her, he said to his dragon. *I know getting her with child would mean she would always be tied to us, but she must come willingly.*

His father wiggled his eyebrows at Aleksei. He didn't even need to send a mental message to know what was on the king's mind.

King Harald turned to Sybil. "I do hope you're enjoying yourself, my dear."

"Oh yes, this is much better than last night." Then she turned red. "I mean, I'm sorry! I didn't mean to imply—"

"No, no need for apologies." King Harald chuckled. "You know, my beloved Natasha, that's Aleksei's mother, she loved all of this. She loved working as the head of the Trust. It was her project, after all. She started it."

"She did?"

"Yes. Of course, we take care of all our citizens here, but Natasha wanted to bring it all together under one umbrella organization." King Harald smiled fondly, as he often did when he spoke of Aleksei's mother. "See, there are people here who need help, too."

Aleksei had to hand it to his father; the old man was sneaky. But then again, that's what made him a good king—he knew how to read people.

"I see that," Sybil said.

The young woman who had handed the baby to Sybil came back, all the while apologizing profusely. Sybil assured her she didn't mind at all and was happy to help. Aleksei couldn't help but feel proud of his mate; she would absolutely make a great queen and mother to their children someday. He just wished she would see it too. Unable to stop himself, he put a hand around her shoulder.

"Aleksei," she whispered. "People might see." But she made no move to shrug him off.

"Then let them see." He leaned down close enough to her ear that he could smell her delicious scent, his nose a hair's breadth away from her soft, smooth skin.

They spent another two hours at the barbecue, talking with everyone, eating the delicious food, and Aleksei even played a traditional Northern Isle game with the kids. When he was defeated by one of the older children, he graciously deferred to the boy, who seemed both shocked and proud that he had defeated the Crown Prince.

"You totally let him win," Sybil whispered to him as he sat beside her on the grass.

He nodded to the boy, who was surrounded by his friends, slapping him on the back and congratulating him. "Let's have our young friend bask in his glory."

Sybil gave him a bright smile that warmed his heart, then leaned her head on his arm as she sank against his side. Aleksei closed his eyes, enjoying the feel of his mate by his side. *Where she belongs.*

"Ahem."

"Yes?" Aleksei said in an annoyed voice. "What is it, Thoralf?"

The Captain of the Dragon Guard's face was drawn into a severe frown. "Your Highness, it's getting late. We should get back to the castle."

Aleksei's spine stiffened. *What is the matter, my friend?* The tension from Thoralf was practically rolling off him.

His Majesty planned this outing last minute, and I'm concerned that we have not prepared the security plans well enough. Thoralf's eyes scanned the area.

"You're doing it again, aren't you?" Sybil said in a dry tone.

"Doing what?"

She tapped the side of her temple. "That mental talk thing. I *know* you are, don't deny it."

Aleksei chuckled. "Fine, you know our secret."

She huffed. "Maybe someday I'll learn it too."

Thoralf cleared his throat again. "Your Highness? The car is waiting."

"Right. You go ahead and secure my father. We will be along shortly." As Thoralf bowed and walked away, Aleksei stood up and offered his hand to Sybil, which she accepted. When he pulled her up, he felt a little cheeky and pulled her to him. "You look beautiful today, did I tell you that?"

"No, I don't believe you have," she said with a mocking pout.

"Well, I am telling you now. Especially when you were holding that baby."

A blush spread over her cheeks. "Aleksei..."

He was desperate to have her alone again. To kiss her, and maybe undress her again, and have her writhing in pleasure as he tasted her. He meant what he had told her last night. "I should—"

A scream interrupted his words and suddenly, his dragon instincts went into overdrive.

"Aleksei!" Sybil's voice was panicked. "What's happening?"

He was already running back toward the tent where the scream had come from. *There.* Three men were standing a few feet from his father and Thoralf. These men, they were dressed in the same white uniforms as the servers, but Aleksei could feel they weren't from here. *Outsiders.* "Father!"

The horror in front of his eyes unfolded in slow motion. One man pointing something at his father, and a sickeningly familiar orange light zoomed toward him. *The Wand.* It hit King Harald with a loud sizzling sound and his father staggered back. Thoralf stepped in front of his father as the second man took out a large weapon, but the captain was too late. The weapon went off, and both Thoralf and King Harald collapsed to the ground.

"No!" Aleksei's heart jumped into his throat and the three men turned to him. The man raised The Wand toward him, but before he could use it, something large—Stein—tackled him to the ground. He dropped the wand, but unfortunately, the third man picked it up and ran away.

Aleksei was torn, but decided to continue running toward his father, stopping his momentum in time to kneel down. "Father ... please ..." He cradled his head gently on his lap, trying to control the expression on his face as he looked at his father's torso, where red bloomed through his shirt.

"So ... cold." King Harald was on the ground, his face ashen. "My ... boy ... you must ..."

"Shh ... don't talk, Father. It's all right. You'll be fine." His throat was constricting so hard he couldn't breathe.

"Your Majesty." Thoralf looked even more horrified. He also had a wound on his arm, but clearly it was already healing. "The bullet went through me and must have ..."

Rage began to pour into his veins. But first he had to take care of King Harald. "Get my Father to the hospital!"

"At once!" Thoralf scooped up King Harald into his arms and quickly made his way out of the Royal Gardens.

Aleksei turned to the attackers. Stein and Rorik had already wrestled both under control. The two men were on their knees as the Dragon Guards held them down, arms behind them. "How did you get in here?" He didn't need to ask who they were. "Who betrayed us?"

One of the men—the one who had used The Wand—craned his head up at him. "Dragon scum." He spat at Aleksei.

Aleksei reacted instantly, landing a blow on the man's cheek so hard he heard the bones crack. "Someone betrayed us. Who? Tell me now and I will make your death quick."

"Does it matter, you abomination?" The man laughed, and Rorik tightened his hold, but he refused to make a sound though his face twisted in pain.

"You." He looked at the other man. "Tell me what you know."

Stein didn't even need a signal from Aleksei as he held that man in a headlock and twisted. The man screamed in agony. "All right!" he gasped when Stein released his head. "It was one of your own. Your cousin."

The words hit him like a ton of stone. At first, he denied it. Erik would never betray them, especially to their mortal enemies. What would he hope to achieve? But why would this man lie?

"It doesn't matter anyway," the first man said with a laugh. "Soon, all of you will be gone! We will decimate this Godforsaken island. Your dear cousin has betrayed you, and now we know your location. We are coming and we will be prepared."

"Aleksei!" Sybil had caught up to him and held his hand. "Oh my God! Your father—"

"He will be fine." But the pit in his stomach grew. Even if King Harald did survive, what kind of life would he live, without his dragon? He knew exactly how that would be and had seen it with his own eyes. But there were so many other things to think about. The betrayal of his cousin. An impending attack. And the safety of his mate. "Take these scum away," he ordered. "Then have the Dragon Navy comb every inch of the Northern Isles to find that third man. He has The Wand and we can't let him get back to the rest of his companions."

Rorik and Stein hauled the two men to their feet and dragged them across the grass.

Finally, he turned to Sybil. "I must take you to safety."

"What? No! Aleksei, you have to—"

He couldn't hear her words. The anger was buzzing in his head, making it hard to think. Later, he couldn't even recall what had happened. All he remembered was pulling Sybil along despite her protests, and commanding Gideon to take her back to the palace and secure her.

Aleksei did remember the last thing he said to his remaining Dragon Guard. "Niklas, go find my *dear* cousin and tell him we need to have a chat."

"And if he resists?"

"Then do what you must."

CHAPTER FIFTEEN

Sybil had never been so sick and anxious in her life. It had been more than twenty-four hours since she'd seen Aleksei. She'd been angry at him for locking her up, but she understood that he had duties and responsibilities to his people.

Still, it wasn't a reason to keep her a prisoner. While Gideon seemed like he was the most reasonable of the Dragon Guards, he was no less loyal and followed his prince's instructions to a T. He had brought her to her room and stood guard outside, and no amount of pleading and begging would get through to him. Finally, she gave up but asked to be put in Aleksei's rooms instead. He had to come back and rest or change clothes at some point, right? She wanted to catch him and make sure he was okay.

And so here she was, all alone in Aleksei's room, laying on his bed. Her heart hurt for him and for King Harald. Every now and then, she would ask Gideon if he had heard any news about the king's condition, but he didn't know either, only that he was still alive and fighting. Even Ursula, when she came in to bring Sybil her meals, simply answered her questions with shrugs and sighs.

Sybil didn't even have the energy to be bored. She was so caught up in her own thoughts. Her phone didn't work, of course, so she didn't even know what was happening outside the Northern Isles. Was everyone back home okay? Did The Knights attack the other clans?

All this uncertainty was driving her crazy. And to think, right before those men attacked, she really was having a good time. The barbecue with the kids and the elderly people had been fun, and more than that, she had seen a side of Aleksei she had never seen before. Kind, caring, and loving to his people. It was a breath of fresh air, and it was almost dizzying the way she found herself being drawn to *this* Aleksei.

Her dragon snorted, as if chiding her: why did it take you this long? She mentally shook her head. She wasn't sure. But all she wanted was to see Aleksei now to comfort and hold him.

This was driving her crazy, and she was ready to shift into her dragon form and break out when the door opened. Her breath caught in her throat. "Aleksei."

His face was drawn into a deep scowl when he walked into the room. It was obvious that he hadn't slept at all, based on the disheveled state of his clothes—the same ones he had been wearing yesterday—and the bags under his eyes. When his gaze crashed against hers, his eyes grew wide. "Sybil? What are you doing here? I told Gideon—"

"He did what you told him," she said. "But I asked to be moved here."

"Why?"

"Why?" she said in an incredulous voice. "You had no plans

of seeing me at all, did you? Otherwise, you'd have realized my room was empty."

His lips drew back into a thin line. "I have been preoccupied, as you can imagine."

"I know that." She tried not to let his dismissive tone hurt her. Aleksei needed her right now and her heart was aching, knowing the pain he was going through. "Please, Aleksei. Sit down and talk to me."

"I don't have time!" he growled. "My father is clinging to life, I found out my only other family has betrayed me and I had to throw him into the dungeon, not to mention, The Knights are probably on their way here now with an army of their own."

"You can't do this to yourself," she said. "You're obviously tired. When was the last time you slept? Or ate? Rest for a bit. Just lie down. You have competent people under you, and I'm sure they'll understand if you need a moment to process things."

"I have had time to process things." His hands clenched at his sides. "One thing at least. You are leaving as soon as the jet is fueled and prepped."

"What? No!" How dare he! "I am *not* leaving!"

"Did you not hear what they said? There is an impending attack! The Knights have known our location for months. We interrogated Erik and he confessed that he gave them all the intel they need for this attack," he said in a bitter voice. "This is no place for you."

Sybil walked to him, facing him toe-to-toe, despite the fact that he towered over her. "This is exactly my place. I can help, Aleksei. Are you forgetting that I'm a dragon too?"

"I would never allow you to risk your life."

"You wanted me to live this life with you, right? Then don't shut me out now."

Aleksei grew quiet, then said, "Then maybe I don't want you in this life."

Her heart dropped to her stomach. He couldn't mean that. *No!*

Her dragon protested, too, with a roar of defiance. *Mine. Mate.*

"No way." She poked a finger on his chest. "You don't get to decide. I have my own mind and my own heart."

Aleksei sighed, turned his back to her, and walked over to his bed. He sat down and dropped his head into his hands. "I realize it was unfair of me to issue you an ultimatum without you knowing what the responsibility a life like mine has. Ruling is not a privilege, but a burden. That's a lesson my father has been trying to teach me all my life. We serve the people, not the other way around."

Tears burned at Sybil's throat as she approached him. She knelt down in front of him and pulled his hands away so she could look into the blue-green depths of his eyes. "Aleksei, please don't take back what you said to me the other day. Don't take back your offer."

"Knowing what could happen, you would still want to be Queen? You would want this burden?"

She laughed. "I'm not saying I want to be Queen. Aleksei, this life wouldn't be a burden. Not to me. Not when I get to have *you*."

His expression was one she could only describe as astonishment. He didn't move, as if he wasn't sure what he had just heard. So, she decided to make it plainer. "Aleksei, I love you. I want to be with you. If that means I'll be Queen, so be it. But I will be your wife and your mate first." She got up and stood between his legs. Leaning down, she brushed his hair back from his face and pressed her lips to his. He remained still for a few seconds, but soon he was responding ardently. His hands planted on her hips, then wrapped around her waist, pulling her down on the bed.

His lips never left hers, like he was savoring her, his tongue teasing and tasting her. He rolled over so he was on top, careful not to crush her with his upper body. He propped himself up, leaning over her. "You acknowledge me as your mate? And accept the mating bond?"

A warmth spread over her. "I do. But," she traced his lips with her finger. "I claim *you* as my mate, too."

He let out a deep growl before he took her mouth in a savage kiss. It was wild, claiming, but freeing at the same time. She knew what it felt like to fly, but it was like she was being launched into the stratosphere. Soaring high above the earth that it was almost dizzying, then free falling. But she wasn't quite falling because she felt a sensation of something wrapping around her like a warm, cozy blanket, and for the first time in her life she had this comforting feeling that she would never be alone again.

When Aleksei released her from the kiss, he looked just as surprised as her. "The bond. You felt it too."

She nodded.

"Sybil ... I never thought ... this is ..."

She couldn't blame him, she felt just as speechless. But, one of them needed to say something. "Aleksei, please ... make love to me now."

The growl of desire that rumbled from this chest was unmistakable. "Sybil. Thank you. For this wonderful gift."

"I feel like I've been waiting my whole life for you, Aleksei." She reached up and pulled him down again, eager to be spoiled by his kisses. And he did spoil her, his kiss passionate and fierce and intense. She never wanted this to end, and she gave a disappointed cry when he moved away, but then let out a gasp when his tongue licked a path down the column of her neck.

He made quick work of her clothes, whipping her sweater over her head and tugging her bra off. As he licked and suckled at her nipples, his hands slid down her jeans and her panties. She felt vulnerable, bared to him under lights, but at the same time it was like her skin was on fire and his touch was the only thing that could soothe her.

"My mate," he murmured against her skin as he moved lower down to her belly and then between her legs.

"Aleksei." She groaned aloud and lifted her hips up to meet his mouth. His hands steadied her, bringing her back down as his tongue did delicious things to her. He was relentless, bringing her to the edge, then backing away just enough to keep her there. When he finally did tease her to orgasm, she swore she went blind briefly from her world exploding around her.

"Please," she panted as she came down from the mind-blowing pleasure. "Don't make me wait any longer."

"As you wish." Aleksei rocked back on his heels and pulled off his shirt. The sight of his bare torso took her breath away, and she couldn't help but groan when he took his pants off. His cock was ready, hard and standing at attention, a pearl of pre-cum beading at the tip. "I'll be as gentle as I can," he whispered as he crawled over her. Nudging her knees apart, he moved between her thighs.

She sighed and closed her eyes. She felt the thick head of his cock pressing against her and she let out a breath, trying to relax her body. Slowly, he moved into her and she opened her eyes to look at him. He seemed deep in concentration as he slipped more and more of himself inside her. When he hit that barrier, he bit his lip.

"I'm sorry, *lyubimaya moya*."

"Oh!"

The pain was brief when he pushed all the way inside her. She knew it couldn't be helped. His body went all tense.

"Aleksei, you feel incredible inside me," she whispered, running her fingers up and down his back. "More. Please, I want it all."

He grunted and slipped his hands under her, raising her hips up. Then, he began to move and she gasped. She thought him being inside her was nice, but now … "Ooh!" The pleasure building inside her was too much. She couldn't believe … nothing could possibly feel like this. Aleksei changed his angle just right so he could brush up against her clit and that sent her yelping and clawing her nails down his back.

"Aleksei! Oh God!"

It was like she was in a dream. But no, this was reality. Aleksei had taken her virginity and was now making love to her. He slid all the way out, and then pushed back into her quickly. The friction was maddening, exhilarating, and almost frustrating because she didn't know how to react or how this would end.

"Sybil," he gasped. "Sybil … Sybil …" He said her name over and over again, as if it was the only word he knew. He shifted her hips again, this time deepening his thrusts into her.

"God!" Sybil cried out when the orgasm hit her. She knew it was coming but still, it was like a hurricane out of nowhere. Her body convulsed involuntarily as the pleasure seemed to hit her over and over again like waves crashing on a rock. She tightened around him and then felt his cock pulse as a sticky warmth filled her. Aleksei thrust into her a few more times, moaning her name as his body shivered, then his movements slowed down.

The tension had broken in the air it seemed and the air went still. Her body protested when he slipped out of her and rolled beside her, but she knew she wouldn't be able to take his weight for too long. His seed, sticky and warm, still coated her thighs and while it seemed like the polite thing to do was get cleaned up, she didn't really care. Plus, they didn't really think about protection or anything so it didn't matter. Nothing else mattered right now except she and Aleksei were truly mates.

She moved up beside him, crawling against his side as his arm came around her to pull her close. She snuggled up to his chest, enjoying the warmth of his skin as she closed her eyes.

Sybil wasn't sure how long they were out. It could have been minutes, it could have been hours. Her mind was clouded from sleepiness. At least it was, until she felt a warm hand move under her rib cage to cup her breast.

Hmmm ... that feels good. But I do wish he would play with my nipples. His thumb and forefinger rolled her nipple, teasing it to hardness.

She moaned. *I wonder how it would feel if he pinched it?* She never understood why some girls liked that. She wasn't into pain or anything but—

Oh wow. "Unngghh ..." She couldn't help herself. That pinch felt *really* good. It sent a zing of pleasure right to her core and she felt herself get wet. *A finger or two down there would feel good too.*

"*Jesus!*" She nearly jolted out of bed when his finger slipped inside her. His thumb found her clit too, and began to stroke it. "Oh! Aleksei, yes."

Do you like that, lyubimaya moya?

Sybil froze. She was pretty sure she could feel his lips sucking at her neck, but she heard his voice. No, wait; his voice echoed *in her head.*

She pulled away from him and turned around. "Did you say that?"

He frowned. "Say what?"

"You ... you asked me if I liked it ... but in my head."

He cocked his head. *Like this?*

"Oh my God!" She scrambled away from him, gathering the sheets around her. "Ohmigodohmigodohmigod." *This couldn't be happening. Can't be happening.*

Ah, but it is. Aleksei raised a brow at her.

"You're really doing it!" she exclaimed.

"You can too," he said. "Try it."

Sybil took a deep breath and closed her eyes. *Like this? Oh my God, I'm doing it! I'm doing it, aren't I?*

He chuckled. "Yes, you are."

Her heart stopped. *What the heck was going on?*

"Isn't it obvious?" he said, slowly crawling toward her. "You are truly my mate now. Thus, you can talk to me through our mental link."

"I ... it's all so ..." She sank against him as he gathered her into his arms. "I—"

"Your Highness!"

They'd been so wrapped up in their discovery that apparently, they didn't hear the door slam open. Thoralf, Gideon, and Niklas barged in, dressed in some type of armor.

"Your Highness! We have news! The—" Thoralf's eyes darted over to Sybil and stopped short.

Holy fucking shit, Aleksei, hang a sock on the door or something next time.

Don't talk to the prince that way, Niklas, Gideon chided.

"Shush!" Sybil covered her ears. "Stop. Please."

"Sybil?" Aleksei asked, looking down at her. "What's wrong."

"Too ... loud. You're all too loud."

What does she mean, too loud? Thoralf asked.

"That's what I mean," Sybil cried. *Poop! I can hear them which means they can hear me! Oh God, don't think about anything, Sybil. Don't think about that time Aleksei went down on you in the pool or how amazing the sex was or—*

"And we're the loud ones?" Niklas said, wincing visibly. "If you're going to start mind speaking, you'll have to learn to stop shouting. And talking about how you and the prince did the nasty. None of us need to know the details." He suddenly smiled. "Though it's nice to know you're finally coming out of that infernal slump you've been on, Aleksei."

"You really can hear us, my lady?" Thoralf asked.

"Yes."

"We are truly mates," Aleksei said proudly. "Sybil and I have completed the mating bond."

"My lady," Thoralf gave a deep bow. "Or should it be, Your Highness?"

"Technically, you call her that after they get married," Gideon said.

"Regardless," Thoralf began. "As mate to our Crown

Prince, the Dragon Guard are in your service. We are pledged to protect you with our very lives."

"Hell, I'm grateful you've finally put that nice bed to use," Niklas said dryly. *I thought your dick would shrivel up and wither off. I even tried to help you a couple of times by sneaking all those women in here—* "Oh shit, she heard that, right?"

"She most certainly did." Sybil's eyes narrowed into razor-thin slits at Aleksei.

Aleksei put his hands up. "I swear, I had Thoralf take those women home as soon as I found them."

"We are *definitely* changing that mattress after we get married," she huffed.

"So, are you saying yes?" Aleksei teased.

"Wait, are you asking? I don't think I heard you ask," she countered.

"Well then—"

"Ahem." Thoralf's face changed into a mask of seriousness. "Your Highness, I really must have your attention. Things have escalated and we need you."

"Of course." He looked down at Sybil, who was still clinging to him. "Let's chat outside. We need to get ready."

The three men bowed and quickly left the room.

"I hope they don't do that all the time," Sybil said wryly. "I plan to be naked a lot in this room."

The rumble from his chest sounded half aroused and half-annoyed. "They'll have to start knocking then." He gave her a quick kiss on the forehead, then slipped out of bed and put his pants on. "When you're dressed and ready, meet me outside the door."

"Of course." Sybil quickly gathered her own discarded clothing and slipped them on, then tried to put some semblance of order to her hair by combing her fingers through it. *Not that it mattered,* she thought with a sigh. It was obvious to everyone what had happened between her and Aleksei. And apparently, she could broadcast it to everyone mentally too.

Giving up on her hair, she went to the door and slipped out into the hallway, where the four men were already deep in conversation.

"And you're certain?" Aleksei asked.

"One of the scouts you sent ahead reported back. He couldn't get too close without being detected but he says a big mass of ships is headed this way."

Aleksei let out what must have been a curse in his language. "All right, let's head to the war room." He turned to Gideon. "I must ask you again for the most important task of all. You must keep my mate and our future queen safe. The Wand is still out there, somewhere here in the Northern Isles and I'm positive that once The Knights have begun their attack, the wielder will be emboldened enough to come out of hiding and try to use it."

"Of course, Your—"

"Hold on, just a minute." Sybil raised her hand. "I'm not going anywhere with him. I'll be headed to this war room with you."

"The war room?" Aleksei asked. "You will do no such thing."

"Of course, I will. I'm your future queen, right? Then I need to do my part to protect the Northern Isles too. You *need* me."

The silence that met her was deafening. Aleksei's face was impassive, but the tension showed in his body. He said a few words in Nordgensprak to the three men, who all bowed then pivoted on their heels, and disappeared down the hallway.

"Aleksei," she began. "You can't mean to lock me away again. Not after last night." She planted her hands on her hips, as if daring him.

"You do not understand." His mood seemed to darken. "Unless I show you."

"Show me what? Aleksei, if The Knights are coming, we don't have time for this."

"Please, Sybil. Will you just let me show you this one thing?" His face was completely serious.

She took a deep, calming breath. "Fine. But I doubt it will change my mind."

"We will see."

He led her away toward another part of the castle. Sybil hadn't really been to many places in here, so she was curious as to where they were going. It seemed to take forever, getting lost in more corridors and hallways. When they reached the end of a long stone corridor, they went down a winding set of stone steps.

"Huh." Sybil's brows knitted together. There was a metal door at the bottom. Aleksei placed his hand on a rock and pushed it aside, revealing a hidden number pad. He punched in a few numbers and the metal door slid open. "What is this place?"

Aleksei remained silent, but led her down the hallway. It looked just like the rest of the castle, plush and richly-appointed, with wood panel walls and carpeting, though the interiors were done in a more feminine style. *What the hell was going on?*

They stopped at one of the doors. "Willa," Aleksei called as he knocked softly. "Willa, it's me. Aleksei."

The door opened slowly, and Sybil's curiosity grew even bigger. A young woman peeked out, her light blue eyes widening as she saw Sybil. "Who is this? Aleksei, I told you, I don't ever want visitors."

"I wanted Sybil to meet you."

"Sybil?" Willa's expression grew suspicious. "Sybil ... Lennox?"

How did this woman know her? "Have we met?"

"I—no!" Her face twisted into anger. "How could you?" she railed at Aleksei. "Of all the people in the world, why *her*? Why did you bring her here?" She tried to claw at Aleksei, and while Sybil's dragon howled in anger, he was able to grab her hands to subdue her.

"I'm sorry, Willa, I really am. But you are a guest here, remember that."

Willa wrenched away from him. "I never wanted to be here! I told you what I wanted, but all you Dragon Alphas somehow get to decide *my* fate because my entire clan is gone." She sobbed into her hands.

"Aleksei, what the hell is going on?" Sybil's anger was bubbling to the surface. "Why do you have this woman imprisoned here?"

"This is not a prison," Aleksei said. "But she's here for her own protection. She may leave anytime she likes, but she knows the one thing we can't allow her to do."

"One thing? I—" *Wait a minute.* This woman knew who she was. And she said her entire clan was gone. A dreaded feeling crept into her stomach, but Sybil knew she had to confirm it herself.

Carefully, she approached the other woman. With the gentlest touch she could manage, she took Willa's hand away from her face. "Willa, please look at me."

The young woman raised her head, then stared up at Sybil defiantly. "Go ahead. You know what I was."

The coldness that began to seep in her veins was practically Arctic. It was Willa's eyes—hollow and lifeless, like there had been something there but now was gone—that gave it away.

"You're a dragon." Another female dragon.

"*Was*," she said, her voice choking. "Was a dragon. But then The Knights attacked and stole The Wand, then killed every last one of us Ice Dragons. They came to us, in the middle of the night and they used The Wand on all of us. It was chaotic and so they didn't see I was still breathing."

"We found Willa, huddled under ... the others," Aleksei said. He sounded like he too, wanted to sob.

Sybil couldn't stop the tears from streaming down her cheeks. "I'm sorry. I'm so sorry."

"I hope you didn't come here to throw me a pity party," Willa said bitterly. "This is why I'm here. I don't want anyone to look at me the way you're looking at me now. Especially *you*. Sybil Lennox. Daughter of Henry Lennox of the Blackstone Dragons. Oh yes, I know about you; how could I not? Even in my clan, I was the only female, also the daughter to the alpha. I thought that maybe, someday, if I ever left that godforsaken place we called home, I could have met you."

"I'm sorry, really, I am." Oh God, she was making this worse. "Aleksei, I—Aleksei?"

But he was gone. Where did he go?

"That *bastard*!" Sybil ran toward the exit as fast as she could, but it was too late. As the door slid into place, the last thing she saw was Aleksei's somber expression.

"Asshole!" she screamed at the door. She banged her fists at the metal, screaming bloody murder, but Aleksei was long gone by now. She'd been outsmarted again; sure, he wanted her to understand why he didn't want The Knights to use The

Wand on her, but also to trap her here. "That's what you think, Prince Jerkface." She would find a way out of here.

She walked back toward Willa, who was standing by the doorway. "What did he mean that you're not a prisoner here? You can walk out anytime?"

"Yes."

"So, there's another exit?"

"Yes."

"Then show me."

"No."

Sybil gritted her teeth in annoyance. "Why not?"

Willa crossed her arms under her breasts. "I'll tell you on one condition."

"What is that?"

"That you help me get what I want. What the alphas are denying me."

"And what is that? Do you need money? A place to stay?" Sybil asked. "I'm sure we can put you up in Blackstone."

"No." Willa's voice shook. "When they found me and I realized that my dragon truly was gone, I begged them to just leave me alone. To let me end my life and join the rest of my clan. That's when they took me here. So," she straightened her shoulders. "Once I show you the other exit and you shift into your dragon form, you have to burn me with your dragon fire."

"No!" Sybil said. Her skin crawled at the horrifying thought.

"Please!" Willa begged, getting down on her knees and wrapping her arms around Sybil's legs. "I can't live like this. You don't know what it's like, walking around feeling like an empty husk all the time. Aleksei is having me monitored 24/7 with this special chip he implanted on my body. If I even try to cut myself or take any pills, it alerts the hospital." She stared up at her with those cold, empty eyes. "I beg you, Sybil. Your dragon fire could kill me in an instant. I just need release from this pain."

"No, Willa, I will not!" Sybil grabbed the other woman and hauled her to her feet. "I swear to you, once this is all over, I'll help you. We'll find a way to get your dragon back. But you have to help me now."

"No!" Willa pulled away from her. "You can watch Aleksei and everyone else suffer, knowing you could have helped them, had you given me what I wanted."

Sybil really did pity this poor, bitter woman, but she understood. "I don't treat life so cheaply," she said. "And my dragon fire—" She stopped. "Holy moly, I'm an *idiot*." She slapped her hand over her forehead. Did Aleksei really think he could keep her trapped here? Rolling up her sleeves, she turned to Willa. "Look, I'm sorry."

"Do not be sorry for my situation," Willa answered coldly.

Sybil felt the burning flame building within her, and her skin began to turn into scales. "No, I mean, I'm sorry for what I'm about to do. This really is a nice place. Hope you weren't too attached to it."

CHAPTER SIXTEEN

Aleksei had always known that one day he would be called upon to lead his people, but just not this soon nor in such a situation. As he stood high above the Cliffs of Skruor and stared into the ocean, he contemplated what was about to happen.

"We will prevail, Your Highness," Thoralf said as he came up behind Aleksei. "Even with their forces, they will be no match against the Dragon Guard and the Great Dragon Navy."

"Our scouts haven't seen any other ships?" Once they knew they were coming, Aleksei gave them the go-ahead to reconnoiter closer to their enemy. The scouts had said they had about forty ships armed with weapons approaching the Northern Isles.

"None. They said that there were no others for miles and miles." Thoralf scratched his thick golden beard. "Seems like a suicide mission. It sounds like their ships outnumber us two to one, but considering the size of one dragon shifter, we would certainly crush them, especially since the wielder of

The Wand is still hiding out somewhere on the island and they don't have a guarantee he'll make it out here in time."

"Which is what worries me." Indeed, Erik must have told them how many Water Dragons lived on the island. Unless ... could Erik have lied, to give them a disadvantage? Aleksei shook his head. No.

His cousin had clearly betrayed them, for his own personal gain. Niklas had easily found Erik at home in his estate just outside Odelia. He was obviously confident that the plan to assassinate the king would go smoothly and no one would be the wiser to his betrayal, which is why he wasn't even trying to hide. It had been easy to knock him out and bring him back to the palace, Niklas had said, as he had been busy with his mistress when the Dragon Guard burst into his room.

Once Erik had woken up in the dungeon and realized that King Harald was alive and the would-be assassins gave him up, the young prince had confessed. The leader of The Knights, Lord Harken, had promised Erik that once King Harald and Aleksei died and Erik became king, he would leave the Northern Isles alone as long as they pledged fealty to The Knights.

"You're a fool, Erik," he had said to his disgraced cousin. "You know they hate us all; they would have killed you and every single one of our people."

Aleksei would have to decide Erik's fate another time. The Knights were approaching, and they had to get ready for the attack.

"Is everyone in position?" Aleksei asked.

"Yes," Thoralf said. "And as you said, all the civilians are safe in the underground shelters. We did have a good amount of volunteers, but we have them in reserve and protecting the shelters. Jarl Solveigson also offered his city estate as an emergency evacuation center and hospital, if necessary."

"Hopefully it will not come to that." But Aleksei knew it was a possibility, and was glad that the Jarl had made such an offer.

"What next?"

"For now, we wait." Based on their movement, Aleksei and Thoralf predicted that The Knights would come from the west. And they were standing right where they would come through after going through the magical veil. The veil itself was not a physical barrier, just a visual one that kept people from the other side from seeing the Northern Isles. But if they knew where to go, they could pass right through the veil without any problem.

"Perhaps you should stay back and make sure everything goes to plan," Thoralf suggested.

"I cannot let you all risk your lives while I stay away from the battle. A leader would never ask his men to do something he himself wouldn't do."

A hand squeezed his shoulder. "You will be a great king someday, Aleksei."

"Someday, my friend," he replied. Not now. Not yet. He refused to think his father wouldn't be able to recover from this.

"Aleksei. There."

Glad for the distraction, he turned to where Thoralf was pointing. A group of ships appeared in the distance and were fast approaching. Based on their trajectory, they knew exactly where to go.

Ready? He knew that the other Dragon Guard and the rest of the Navy were waiting on the beach below for his signal. They all sent him an affirmative, their voices echoing in his head. He waited until the first line of ships came closer. *Attack!*

He wasted no time; leaping off the cliff, he shifted into his dragon form, hurtling down toward the beach, then suddenly veering upwards as his long wings flapped to send him soaring up to the air.

The rest of his men were already in the water. Members of the Great Dragon Navy were the fiercest warriors in the land. And, unlike other navies in the world, they didn't need any ships or weapons; they *were* the ships, their bodies and claws the weapons. Over twenty fully-shifted water dragons were swimming toward their enemies, ready to face them head-on.

I'll take the lead ship, he told them, indicating the large water craft in front. *And you take your positions and attack at will.*

Aleksei dove straight into the ocean and swam straight for his ship. On land, his dragon was unwieldy and clumsy, while in the air it was merely capable. But, here in the water, it was home. Its body moved with the grace of a dancer, slicing through water quickly and efficiently. The boat was right ahead, so his dragon picked up its speed, seemingly to take it head on. When the ship began firing missiles, the dragon dodged them easily.

As soon as the boat was at the perfect distance, Aleksei maneuvered his dragon to the right, then under, curling the rear part of his long, serpentine body around the ship's hull, then crushed it in half. The sound of metal crunching was deafening, and as soon as Aleksei was satisfied that the boat was disabled, he released it and swam ahead.

All around him, the Dragon Navy was making quick work of their enemies. There were more ships behind, but judging from their progress, their side would soon prevail. Aleksei swam to the surface, bursting out from the waves, his wings pushing him up until he was airborne. As he flew high up, he felt something brush against one of his fins.

What the devil—

He turned back. There was something small, flying toward the mainland. Using his dragon senses, he could see it was some kind of flying machine. Another one whizzed by. And then another one. A drone?

The loud buzzing sound made him turn his head, and when he saw what was coming, he quickly dove back toward the ocean, then looked up.

The sky was nearly covered with what seemed like hundreds of drones as they flew overhead. All heading toward the mainland.

No!

This was what he feared; what his instinct had been telling him. In the ocean, the Water Dragons were unstoppable. But in the air ... they had provisions and weapons for air attacks, but not for something like this. The swarm of drones moved as one, making a beeline for the Isles. And who knew what they carried? Biological weapons? Missiles? Bombs?

Thoralf, you take care of the battle. I must get back. He barely heard the reply as he pushed his dragon's body forward, swimming harder than he'd ever done in his whole life. Rorik and Gideon had stayed behind on the beach, but they were still too far away for him to contact through their mental link. He had to find a way to warn everyone.

He pushed and pushed, finally, bursting out of the water to try and stop the drones himself. His dragon's body hurtled into the air, striking a couple of them down, but they were too fast and too numerous. He saw a few of the drones break away from the group, probably malfunctioning from the knock he gave them. A whirring sound came from one of them, and he saw its belly open, and something fell out—a round metal ball of some sort. When whatever it was hit the ocean, it exploded, sending a spray of water bursting upward.

Aleksei's heart slammed into his ribcage. There wasn't much around the Cliffs of Skruor, maybe a fishing village or two, so he knew the drones would probably head right toward the capital city where they could do the most damage.

Without further thought, he pushed his body even more. As he focused his sights on the mainland, he saw something approaching. Something large and shimmering like gold.

Sybil.

He was a fool to think he could entrap her at the palace with Willa. He should have found another way to keep her safe. Now, the stakes were higher. And—

The fire was blinding, white-hot, and spreading out over the ocean. The golden dragon hovered over the water, its great maw spread open as flames continued to shoot out, burning the approaching drones. The burned-out pieces dropped into the ocean at once. As the dragon stopped to take a breath, it veered right, and the rest of the drones continued its path toward the Isles. The dragon made a U-turn and followed the hoard, then let out another stream of fire.

Aleksei followed suit and when he was near enough, he called to her through their link. *Sybil! What are you doing? You should have stayed—*

Kinda busy here! Her dragon let out another stream of fire, sending a few more drones to the ground. It continued to chase the hoard as Aleksei chased Sybil. *But don't think we're not going to talk about how you trapped me down there.* Another stream of fire. *You are in such big trouble, mister!*

Aleksei didn't know whether to laugh or get angry. But, it

was obvious she had been right; they really did need her. *All right, lyubimaya, what do you need? Gideon and Rorik are on the beach. What can we do to assist you?*

There's too many of them. And I need to recharge for a few seconds before each breath. Plus, we don't know if those drones can fight back or if they've called for some type of backup.

We will flank and protect you, and keep you safe. Based on their distance, he should be near enough to the two remaining Dragon Guard. *Gideon and Rorik! Do what you can to assist my mate. I'll be right beside you.*

Within minutes, two dragons were fast approaching them. They split up, then flew right by Sybil's dragon, flanking each side. As she stopped to breathe, Rorik and Gideon spread out, using their tails to knock as many drones as they could until she was ready again.

Aleksei was getting ready to join them, to take the rear when he felt his instincts going haywire. Of course, it wouldn't be this easy or simple. And just as he thought, he spied from the corner of his eye a figure on the ground. He didn't know why, but he knew who it was. *The third assassin.*

He pulled at his dragon's body with all his might, veering it away from Sybil and headed straight toward the beach. There he was. The man raised his arm, The Wand in his hand, pointed right at Sybil.

No!

Aleksei didn't even try to control his speed as he hurtled toward the beach. The last thing he saw before his dragon's body went tumbling down was the look of surprise on the assassin's face, right before his dragon's head knocked him to the ground.

Aleksei quickly shifted back to his human form, and reached out to grab the assassin as they rolled around the sand. He maneuvered his human body so he ended up on top, his hands squeezed around the man's throat as he gasped for air. He wanted to kill this man, but instead, he settled for a blow to the head that knocked him out.

"Aleksei," Rorik said, placing a hand on his shoulder. "We'll take care of him. Go see to your mate."

"Sybil? Where is she? What happened to the drones?"

"They're gone. Sybil stopped them. Your mate is one kick-ass chick," Gideon said with a laugh. "Remind me never to piss her off."

"She's going to be your queen someday, so you better not," Aleksei warned. "Not if you like your hide intact."

The sound of wings flapping and a strong gust of wind made them look up. A dragon flew overhead. From the scars on the long, scaly body, Aleksei could tell that it was Stein.

A few drones broke off from the hive and are headed to the city. Stein's gravelly voice sounded alarmed, a rarity for the normally stoic Water Dragon. *I need—* The mental link broke off as he flew farther and farther away.

Aleksei glanced at the man on the ground, who was still out cold. "Gideon, take care of this bastard. And Rorik, go help Stein."

"At once, Your Highness."

He knew he could trust his friends, so he went off in search of his mate. "Sybil!" he called. "Sybil, where are you?"

"Aleksei!" a small voice squeaked. "I'm here. Over here. Come quick."

Turning to the sound of Sybil's voice, he strode to the group of bushes to his left. He nearly jumped out of his skin when Sybil's head popped out from behind a leafy branch.

"Sybil?"

"Is anyone with you?" She looked around, and when she saw there was no one, sighed in relief. "Hand me your shirt."

"My shirt?"

"I'm naked!" she cried. "Very naked under here."

Aleksei bit his lip to keep from laughing, and dutifully did as she asked. She yanked the shirt from his hand, then disappeared. A few seconds later, she emerged wearing his shirt, which hung down below her knees.

"Now," she put her hand on her hips. "You better get ready, mister, because I'm about to give you an ear blistering that will—hmm!"

He silenced her with his mouth. He'd give her a chance to chew him out later, but for now, he just needed her. To feel her in his arms and to kiss her, so he knew that this was real. That she was here and alive and with him. His dragon sighed in contentment as he felt the bond pulling them together and making him feel warm inside.

"Aleksei," she whispered when he pulled away. "What ... you ..."

"I can bring you up to speed later. You can even 'blister my ear' all you want. But first, I must apologize to you."

"A-a-apologize?"

"You were right. I shouldn't have locked you up like that, and you had every right to be here, to protect our people and fight by my side."

"I do?" She seemed confused.

"Yes. Forgive me. As your mate, it's my instinct to protect you and keep you safe. But you are no child, and you will be Queen someday."

"And don't forget, I kind of saved your ass."

He chuckled. "Yes indeed. You saved my ass. And the entire kingdom. And I will make sure they know this."

"Aleksei," she said, her expression softening. "I told you, I don't need any of that." She wrapped her arms around his waist and pulled him close. "I just need *you*."

He didn't know why he got so lucky. To have a fierce, loyal, protective, and beautiful mate like her. "Sybil, I love you." And now, he would finally get to do what he'd been meaning to do. He got down on one knee, then reached into his back pocket. "Will you marry me?"

Sybil's silvery eyes grew to the size of dinner plates as she looked down at the ring between his fingers. "Holy moly! That thing is enormous! You probably had that thing locked up with like, five guards or something. When did you find time to get it?"

"I had my father take it out of Royal Treasury as soon I told him about you right before we got here. He gave it to me when I arrived and I've been carrying it around ever since. This was my mother's. My father had it made just for her after I was born." The stone was a twelve-carat blue-green diamond surrounded by smaller white ones. "Do you know, despite the fact that the official color of the Royal Family is blue-green, this is the only diamond of this color we've ever found in the quarry? My mother said it was special and had it fashioned into a ring. My father said she'd only worn it once and then put it away."

"Why?"

"It was beautiful, she had said. But something about it didn't feel right and that I was a special gift enough; she didn't need anything else. She mentioned that maybe one day, there would be another future queen who would deserve it."

"Aleksei ..." Her eyes shimmered with tears. "I don't know what to say."

"Say yes." He took her hands in his. "Please."

She stared into his eyes, and the way she looked at him took his breath away. Like there was no one else in the world around them. Like she had poured every inch of love she felt and was handing it to him.

"Then yes, Aleksei. I will marry you."

EPILOGUE

SEVEN MONTHS LATER...

"I know I say this each time, Dutchy," Riva said. "But you really have outdone yourself."

The fox shifter gave her a smile. "Well, this isn't just a royal wedding, but a coronation, too. I had to pull out all the stops."

"Can I look at myself now?" Sybil asked. She still had her back turned to the mirror as she stood on the small dais. Although she'd already seen the designs and fitted pieces of the gown, this would be the first time she would see the entire outfit and herself fully made-up.

Dutchy beamed at her. "Go ahead."

Sybil held her breath as she turned around. "I …" She was speechless. The gown really was spectacular. Rather than going for the usual white gown, Dutchy had insisted the dress be gold and bronze. Sybil was worried it would be too much, but she trusted her friend. It wasn't garish at all. Instead, the colors were muted, and the rich embroidery and Spanish lace along the bodice, sleeves, and neckline made for elegant embellishments. The tulle and taffeta skirt had a monarch hemline—of course—and a long train that would trail down the Royal Chapel beautifully. Her hair had been done in a simple bun, and a matching tulle veil was attached. Her head was left unadorned, as right after the marriage ceremony, she would have to wear the queen's crown. *I just hope I'm worthy of it.*

Although they were able to thwart The Knights' attack and secure The Wand—with the Dragon Council keeping it in a secret location—the battle wasn't without its casualties. Sybil still felt guilty about the dozen or so stray drones that had made their way to Odelia. While Stein and Rorik were able to stop most of them, three had reached the city and destroyed half a dozen buildings before they could reach them. There were some casualties and serious injuries, including to Stein, who had used his own body to block an explosive that was about to hit one of the evacuation centers. Aleksei assured her that it wasn't her fault, and that she should instead focus on the entire country that she had saved instead of those they had lost.

And then of course, there was King Harald. The surgeons were able to save him, but The Wand had done its job; the king's dragon was gone and he was human now. Which is why he decided to abdicate and name Aleksei as his successor. The formal abdication took place the previous morning, to make for a smoother transition.

Sybil and Aleksei were worried that he would fall into a depression or madness at the loss of his dragon, but surprisingly, he was taking it well. "Dragon or not," he had told her one afternoon when the two of them were having tea, "I have so much to live for, now that you are here. Our kingdom must look to the future."

The thought of being queen made Sybil nervous. She was 100 percent sure about being Aleksei's wife, but the role of queen, she was iffy about. Though the Northern Isles was an absolute monarchy with advisers and ministers and the role of queen really more ceremonial; but still, she didn't know what she would do after getting married. Aleksei and King Harald assured her that she could do whatever she wished, but she knew she wasn't just going to stand around and smile and cut ribbons. She wanted to make a difference and to help people, especially those they had lost.

"You look beautiful, princess," Hank said as he entered the dressing area of Sybil's guest suite in the palace. His smile was wide, but his eyes wistful. "I mean, I guess I should say, 'Queen'?"

"Dad!" Sybil hopped off the dais and ran to her father, enveloping him in a hug. "And no, you can still call me princess." She felt the tears stinging her eyes and her father's arms surrounded her.

When she and Aleksei decided to wait for spring for their wedding—to give the people of the Northern Isles enough time to mourn the dead, recover from the attack and so that both Penny and Catherine could give birth and travel with the babies—she thought it was too long. But the time had passed too quickly and she couldn't believe her wedding really was here and she would be living in the Northern Isles from now on. Sure, she was still welcome at home, but she couldn't just jet back to Blackstone anytime she wished once she was officially Queen of the Northern Isles.

"You know you'll always be my princess, right?" the hitch

in Hank's voice made her sniff back the tears she'd been fighting.

"I know, Dad," she said. "I know."

"You're going to ruin your makeup," Riva said, but she was also dabbing at her eyes.

"You look beautiful, princess." Hank turned to his mate. "Both of you do."

A discreet cough made them break away. "Sybil." Amelia had entered the room. She looked gorgeous wearing her green and blue matron of honor gown. "You have a visitor."

"Is it Aleksei?" Riva frowned. "I told him no seeing Sybil until the ceremony." It seems that Riva was enforcing her twenty-four hour rule, despite the fact that Aleksei was practically the king of this country and this was his palace. Yesterday, she counted down to the second, dragging Sybil off to her rooms, much to the annoyance of Aleksei.

Amelia laughed. "Not at all. I don't think he'd want to cross you, Aunt Riva. It's Aleksei's dad. Can he come in?"

"Oh." Sybil straightened her dress. "Of course. I asked him to come see me before the ceremony."

"You're all ready," Dutchy proclaimed. "I'll take my place with the girls." Aside from being her dress designer, she asked the fox shifter to be one of her bridesmaids.

"Say hi to Ian for me," Sybil teased. His Grace had been invited to be a groomsman and was Dutchy's partner in the wedding line-up. "Of course, there're other dragons around here, you know."

Dutchy rolled her eyes and swatted her hand at Sybil playfully. "Ugh, you have *one* coffee date with a dragon, and you never hear the end of it."

"I thought you said he was cute," Amelia added.

"Yeah, but we're just friends, I swear." Dutchy gathered her things. "Nothing going on there. Never happened and never will. Anyway, see you on the other side." With a wave, she and Amelia left the room, leaving through the side entrance that led to the sitting room.

Sybil didn't want to say it out loud, but she was glad Dutchy wasn't falling for Ian's charms. Being with her fated mate was one of the most amazing and beautiful things in the world; she understood that now. She wanted the same for Dutchy, who had become one of her closest friends in the last couple of months. Dutchy was funny, lively, talented, but also kind and compassionate. She deserved someone who would love and cherish only her, and not the fickle dragon duke with the wandering eye.

"Sybil?" the former King Harald called softly as he entered through the main door. "Aleksei said you requested to see me before the ceremony?" He approached her, a worried look on his face. "Is everything all right? What's the matter, my dear?"

"I'm all right, Your Majesty," Sybil said with a curtesy. Her mother followed suit and her dad bowed.

"Please, no need for such formalities. I'm not king anymore not since I formally abdicated yesterday," he said, then turned to Sybil. "And, my dear, I told you, when we are alone to address me as—"

"Pappa." Sybil finished. "Anyway," she looked at her parents and Harald. "Aleksei and I discussed and decided that I should tell you the good news, before we all get caught up in the wedding and coronation."

"Tell us what—" Riva's eyes went wide and she put her hand over her mouth. "Sybil!"

Sybil laughed. She never could hide anything from her mother. "Mom, Dad, Pappa: Aleksei and I are going to have a baby." It was early yet, but they couldn't deny it. A few days ago, they both heard it—the sound of the beating heart of their child, deep in her belly.

Riva let out a cry and both Hank and Harald whooped in joy. "My baby!" Riva exclaimed, wrapping her in another fierce hug.

"My dear Sybil," Harald began. "You've ... you've made me so happy."

The tears of joy and the light in Harald's eyes were so real, Sybil wanted to cry. Despite the former king's insistence that he wasn't depressed over his dragon's loss, Sybil could see the sadness in his eyes and that some days, his smile wasn't quite genuine.

Today though, it was like the old King Harald was back and she knew she and Aleksei made the right decision to tell him now. Sybil, after all, knew how deep the depression could go, having spent time visiting Willa in the last few months. Or tried to, anyway, as the former Ice Dragon still refused visitors.

"Look at us, crying like old women." Hank cleared his throat. "Well, now that you're getting married in an hour, I suppose I don't have to get my shotgun anymore."

"Dad!"

The wedding and coronation had been beautiful. *No*, Aleksei thought, *it had been perfect*. Of course, they could have been married in their pajamas, and it would still have been perfect. As long as Sybil was his wife and queen, he would have been happy.

But, he understood that his country needed this, after what they had suffered. A royal wedding and welcoming a new queen would lift everyone's spirits. The wedding, then the coronation had taken place in the Royal Chapel, which was followed by a carriage ride to the palace. It seemed everyone in the Northern Isles had filled the streets of Odelia to greet their new King and Queen.

Aleksei tried to convince his father not to abdicate, but he was determined. "A dragon must rule," King Harald had said. "And besides, you're ready, my son. With your mate at your side, you will breathe new life into our kingdom and take it into the future."

Despite his facade, Aleksei knew the loss of his dragon hurt much deeper than he had let on, which is why he wanted to tell him the good news as soon as possible. When he returned from talking with Sybil, he came into the Crown Prince's rooms with tears in his eyes, so speechless that he could only embrace his son. Aleksei had hoped that a grandchild would help anchor his father's sanity and keep him from spiraling into depression.

The celebration after the ceremony and coronation was small and simple by royal standards, as they didn't want anything too extravagant for themselves. Instead of having an opulent reception, they decided to share as much as they could with the people of the Northern Isles, and the entire main street leading up to the palace had been turned into a street fair with lots of entertainment and free food and refreshments for anyone who could come.

But everyone who was important was here. Sybil's entire family and all her close friends had arrived from Blackstone and other parts of the world. He didn't invite any of the other alphas, aside from Ian MacGregor, or members of the Dragon Council as he wasn't sure he was ready to reveal their secret to them and the rest of the world. There was going to be another reception at Blackstone Castle the following week, and that was the "official" celebration, at least for the rest of the world and the Dragon Alliance. Frankly, despite the bother of all this wedding business, he couldn't wait to rub Matthias Thorne's nose in the fact that he got Sybil and she was carrying his heir. Petty, yes, but he was King now and he could be allowed such things every now and then.

On his side, the ministers and advisers who would soon be serving under him, plus the noble and dragon families of the Northern Isles were also in attendance. He had even spotted Jarl Solveigson and his daughter. He couldn't very well not invite them, especially with all the people they had saved before and after the attack. Aleksei had his doubts about Lady Vera, and was worried that she might upset Sybil, so he asked the Dragon Guard to make sure she didn't try to ruin their day. Much to his surprise, Lady Vera seemed subdued and even curtsied to Sybil as they came down the receiving line.

"What are you thinking of?" Sybil asked as they sat on the dais in the middle of the ballroom. She had been watching the antics of their flower girl and ring bearer—Cassie Walker and Grayson Lennox—as they ran around the ballroom, sliding around in their socks on the smooth floor.

I'm thinking of how I'd like to be alone with my wife now. When she blushed, he clucked his tongue mentally. *Am I still doing that to you? I must not be doing something right.*

She giggled. "Oh, you're doing everything right, my King." Sybil was getting better at not broadcasting her thoughts to other dragons nearby, but there was just too many of them around in the room, which is why she avoided using it for now.

He lowered his voice. "As King, my first proclamation is that this party is over, at least for us, so that I can go make love to my Queen." He slipped an arm around her waist. "I need you, Sybil."

Her lips parted and gaze went half-lidded. "Then what are we waiting for?"

The party was in full swing, and with a signal to Rorik, they were able to slip away. Sybil laughed as they chased each other down the hallway like a couple of children. When they got to their rooms—their new private suites as King and Queen—Thoralf was there, waiting for them.

"Your Majesty." He kneeled down and kept his head bowed.

"On your feet, my friend," Aleksei said. "You are no longer Captain of the Guard."

"Aleksei!" Sybil admonished. "You can't do that! Thoralf is your friend! He's loyal and good and—"

"Sybil," Aleksei said gently. "Thoralf asked to be relieved of his duty as captain. But he will remain part of the guard. Rorik will replace him."

"Is this true?" Sybil asked. "I know you've felt guilty all these months about King Harald, but you couldn't have known that would happen."

"But I should have, my lad—I mean, Your Majesty." His face was drawn into a serious expression. "As Captain of the Guard, it should have been me. I pledged to protect the king and I failed."

"No!" She tugged at his arm. "Aleksei, you can't possibly accept his resignation."

"Like, I said, he's not resigning." Aleksei sighed. Sybil couldn't understand, so he would do his best to explain. "I have released Thoralf from his duty as captain—temporarily —so that he may go on a quest."

"A quest?"

"I requested it, Your Majesty," Thoralf explained. "With Gideon's help, I have found some evidence that there is a way to reverse the effects of The Wand."

Sybil gasped. "There is?"

"Gideon's not certain ... the texts are vague, but there might be."

"And Thoralf asked that he be allowed to go and find this cure," Aleksei added.

"I must, to restore my honor." Thoralf's tone was serious.

She let out a deep sigh. "I suppose ... I mean, if you could, that would be great, but you're a good friend to my husband. A brother, practically. We will miss you. Please," she reached out to squeeze his hand, "come back, whether or not you find a cure."

"I ... cannot promise you, but I will do my best." He bowed again. "I must go, but I wanted to congratulate you and tell you how deeply grateful I am to you, Queen Sybil."

She blinked. "Me?"

Thoralf gave her a sad smile. "You have brought so much happiness to the kingdom, and most importantly, my friend." He glanced at Aleksei. "I always knew you would be a good king, Aleksei. But with her at your side, I know you will be a great one." He gave a final bow before he left and walked away from them.

"Do not be sad, Sybil," Aleksei soothed. "I'm sad that my friend has to leave, but honor is important to Thoralf. Whether or not he finds a way to restore my father, I think it's vital he go and do this."

"If you say so."

Now, he steered her into their bedroom. *On to more important things.*

"Aleksei!" she laughed when he picked her up and threw her over his shoulder.

"I've always wanted to do this," he confessed as he walked them into the room.

"And you waited this long because ..."

He dropped her into the middle of the bed. "Because I didn't think you would enjoy it this much, *lyubimaya moya.*" Even now, he could see the desire in her eyes, blazing bright like the flame of her dragon. He shrugged off his jacket and began to undress.

Slowly, she reached behind her to unzip her dress, then pulled the front down, baring her breasts to him. He let out a soft growl, watching as the rosy pink tips hardened under his gaze. "Sybil." He crawled over to her, reaching out to release her hair, letting it tumble down her shoulders like an ebony waterfall. He kissed her, full and deep. *I love you.*

And I love you. He heard it almost every day from her, but the words still made his heart skip a beat. She was truly his, mind, body, and soul. Every day the mating bond grew stronger, and now, as she carried his child, he knew that it could never be broken.

Mine. Mate. Finally. Truly.

He tugged at the rest of her dress impatiently, nearly ripping it off her in his haste to feel her naked skin against his. He touched her everywhere, their minds linked so intimately he knew what she liked and what pleased her. And when he made love to her, he did it slowly, savoring the feel of her around him. It was the most beautiful feeling in the world to be connected to her in every way. He brought her to orgasm again and again, until she was begging for him to come inside her.

He cried out her name as she clasped around him, milking

him and making him shudder in pleasure as he spilled his seed inside her.

"My Queen," he whispered as he collapsed on top of her.

"Your *wife*," she corrected. "And first and foremost, your mate."

"I'll call you whatever you want," he answered back. "As long as you are *mine*."

It's **not quite** the end!
I have a special extended epilogue available for my newsletter readers

It happens a few more months into the future.

And we see a glimpse of how Sybil and Aleksei's life as king and queen.

Of course, I may give you a sneak peek of upcoming books.

(Like what happens to certain grumpy Dragon Guard. You'll never guess who I'm planning to pair him up with!)

Get it by signing up for my newsletter here:
http://aliciamontgomeryauthor.com/mailing-list/

You'll get access to ALL the bonus materials from all my books and my **FREE** novella **The Last Blackstone Dragon.**

AUTHOR'S NOTES

WRITTEN ON SEPTEMBER 17, 2018

I can't believe the Blackstone Mountain Series has come to an end. Originally, it was going to end with Luke's story and the girls would have their own spinoff, but I just couldn't Blackstone yet.

Thank you so much for sticking with me throughout this saga. I hope you enjoyed all their stories. And if you you enjoyed my books, please do leave me a review. As you know, I'm a self-published author and I'm doing this mostly on my own. Reviews help me know what you like (and what you don't like), but they also help other people make their buying decisions. Even a less than stellar review can help ensure people who only want to read my books will buy it.

So, a little bit of background on the story:

When I started writing Blackstone Mountain, I knew where I wanted to begin and where I wanted to end. Actually, the story begins even BEFORE The Last Blackstone Dragon (Hank and Riva's story—FREE btw). I told you about my fascination with robber barons and how Lucas Lennox was a dragon shifter/robber baron character. However, going even further back, I had a vague idea of what happened with Anastasia Lennox and Silas Walker (and I definitely knew the dragon would be female) and why the Lennoxes were kicked out of the Dragon Alliance, but didn't have the story tied up.

It was right around when I started Ben's story (The Blackstone Bear) that the idea began to form in my head. What if Anastasia was running away from an arranged marriage? Maybe it was another dragon—and what if he were a prince?

Then, inspiration struck—Sybil needed a mate, someone who could handle her and unexpected. BOOM. Aleksei the dragon prince came to mind (and boy, oh boy, did Sybil basically claim him!). I planted the story of Anastasia and Silas in The Blackstone She-Bear. Honestly, it was one of my favorite scenes to write!

Hmmm ... maybe I'll write a short story with Anastasia and Silas. Or maybe I'll finally get around to writing Lucas Lennox's story of how he met his Swedish countess (whose name happens to be Sibella). Think I should do it? Let me know by dropping me a line at alicia@aliciamontgomeryauthor.com Or maybe you want me to move on? I have so many more stories to tell. I have Dutchy's story, J.D.'S story, Cordy's story, and now I know I'll probably have to write about the Dragon Guard, the Silver Dragons, Air Dragons, Rock Dragons, Sand Dragons, and let's not forget the wolves of Lykos! Which one should I do next? Let me know!

But for now, I'm going to be leaving Blackstone for just a bit and I'll be going back to True Mates. I'm working on Jackson's story, but I won't spoil it anymore - you'll just have to read it when it comes out on December 4, 2018.

All the best,
Alicia

ABOUT THE AUTHOR

Alicia Montgomery has always dreamed of becoming a romance novel writer. She started writing down her stories in now long-forgotten diaries and notebooks, never thinking that her dream would come true. After taking the well-worn path to a stable career, she is now plunging into the world of self-publishing.

facebook.com/aliciamontgomeryauthor
twitter.com/amontromance
bookbub.com/authors/alicia-montgomery

Printed in Dunstable, United Kingdom